Dermot Bolger was b[...] [...] four novels, *Night Shift*, which received the AE Memorial Award, the controversial, bestselling *The Journey Home*, which was shortlisted for the *Irish Times*/Aer Lingus Irish Literature Award, *The Woman's Daughter*, which received the Macaulay Fellowship, and *Emily's Shoes*. All are published by Penguin. His first play, *The Lament for Arthur Cleary*, one of the major hits of the 1989 Dublin Theatre Festival and the 1990 Edinburgh Festival, received the Stewart Parker BBC Award, an Edinburgh Fringe First and the 1990 Samuel Beckett Award for best first play seen in Britain, and it has been broadcast on BBC Radio 4. His other plays include *The Tramway End* (two one-act plays staged by the Gate Theatre in Dublin) and *One Last White Horse* (staged by the Abbey Theatre on their Peacock stage), which are published together as *A Dublin Quartet* by Penguin. The author of five volumes of poetry, Dermot Bolger was, for the fifteen years of its existence, the publisher and editor of the Raven Arts press – one of Ireland's most radical publishers – and is now executive editor of New Island Books. He has edited such anthologies as *The Picador Book of Contemporary Irish Fiction* and *The Bright Wave – An Tonn Gheal* (which received An Duais Bhord Na Gaelige) and is currently a member of the Arts Council of Ireland and chairman of MusicBase, the information and resource centre for contemporary popular Irish music.

DERMOT BOLGER

NIGHT SHIFT

PENGUIN BOOKS

PENGUIN BOOKS

Published by the Penguin Group
Penguin Books Ltd, 27 Wrights Lane, London W8 5TZ, England
Penguin Books USA Inc., 375 Hudson Street, New York, New York 10014, USA
Penguin Books Australia Ltd, Ringwood, Victoria, Australia
Penguin Books Canada Ltd, 10 Alcorn Avenue, Toronto, Ontario, Canada M4V 3B2
Penguin Books (NZ) Ltd, 182–190 Wairau Road, Auckland 10, New Zealand

Penguin Books Ltd, Registered Offices: Harmondsworth, Middlesex, England

First published in Ireland and the USA by Brandon Book Publishers 1985
Reissued by The Raven Arts Press, Dublin, 1989
Published in Penguin Books 1993
1 3 5 7 9 10 8 6 4 2

Copyright © Dermot Bolger, 1985, 1989
All rights reserved

The moral right of the author has been asserted

The author would like to acknowledge a special thanks to Mr Steve McDonagh

Printed in England by Clays Ltd, St Ives plc

Except in the United States of America, this book is sold subject
to the condition that it shall not, by way of trade or otherwise, be lent,
re-sold, hired out, or otherwise circulated without the publisher's
prior consent in any form of binding or cover other than that in
which it is published and without a similar condition including this
condition being imposed on the subsequent purchaser

For June, Deirdre and Roger

Part One

One

H E WATCHED the superior smirk of the chargehand's arse vanish down the concrete path between the screeching machines and waited for Frankie's nod. Checking the short man's progress down the factory floor by the anonymous cries of "Get out of that hole!" and "Stop walking in that trench!" which followed him from behind the machines, Donal quickly slipped the inch of twisted wire into the delicate flux he was pressing down into the compressor. Behind him Dan was slowly pumping a trolley up under a full pallet of welding rods. The old man's skin was as rusted as the stacked trays. He had probably spent as long working in the place. Donal knew he was neutral in everything as if he existed in a parallel world to the rest of the factory. Where the long tubes of light hung under the spider structure of girders the night shift was slowly being spun out. The old man moved past pulling the trolley, deliberately ignoring the youth's actions. Donal squeezed the twin handles of the machine downward as if he were drawing two long invisible threads towards his body. From the top of the machine the heavy steel periscope descended to cover the lid of the compressor. The needle behind the cracked glass circle above him spun upward, reluctantly at first, and then, as the loose flux began to solidify under the intense pressure, with a swift ascending curve. When the needle touched seventy tons he released both handles. They snapped back, the periscope shot up, and from the hole in the centre of the metal surface before him a small rounded slug of packed flux began to rise from the metal depths of the compressor. It was black and quickly stiffening, shaped like a pint with no head.

The operator of the main machine was a squat muscular country-man with a basin-shaped hair-cut. He was newly promoted and nervous of the responsibility. He watched Donal with an intent gaze as the young man placed the row of fresh slugs on the strip of guttering used as a loader. The operator swung the guttering around and pushed the slugs down the gleaming steel stomach of his machine, using an iron club to pound them tightly in. At the far end of the machine Frankie was loading small slender rods into the hodder, having twisted one slightly. They stood back as the operator pressed the button and the machine began to fire the rods out, now coated in a burnt crust of flux, at the sheet of metal that broke their fall down onto the endless orange-peel of the conveyor belt. At the far end of the belt Milo and Jimmy waited, smoking, with empty rusting trays in their hands.

"I closed my eyes, drew back the foreskin, to see for certain, what I thought I knew," Milo's voice rose over the noise.

Within seconds the machine jammed with a high-pitched choking whine and shuddered to a halt. Duckarse came racing back down the path, his face blazing with anger, his eyes darting suspiciously from man to man.

"What was in that last slug, Donal?" the operator demanded.

"I think they call it flux, Joe," Donal replied, moving up to join Frankie who was cheerfully leaning on a sweeping brush near the mixer.

The operator swung the machine open and began to peel away the hardened coat of flux from the mouth of the door with his knife. Duckarse watched him with his hands bunched deep in his brown coat pockets.

"Donal, did you see anything in the flux?" he asked.

"I've seen worse in good restaurants."

"Listen," Jimmy said, strolling over from the conveyor belt to join them. "We all know that Joe can't operate the bloody machine. He's a bog Arab. He's soft up where it counts. In the bleeding head. That's the fifth breakdown this shift. Sure we're all pissed off."

The chargehand looked around, surveying the machines, and then eyed the bunch of men.

"If that machine is being tampered with there will be men going

10

out of this factory on their arse, work-to-rule or no work-to-rule, union or no union. Right!"

He turned his back on them and bent over to talk to Joe. The pair of them were leaning forward and peering down the barrel of the machine like a gun crew on a ship. Jimmy drew the two young men back and said quietly, "Would you look at them. It looks like a queers' picnic. They must have half a brain between them. I remember the first week Duckarse got his brown coat. The general manager came down with a party of businessmen to show them the workings of this grand little circus. Ned used to work this machine before they pensioned him off and he'd always be transferring the spittle from one corner of his mouth to the other. Anyway the machine was stopped and we were all busy pretending to be working but there wasn't a bother on Ned. There he was, one hand in his pocket, peeling away the hard flux from the machine with a knife in the other and transtransferring the spittle. Then finally after they had been standing watching him for a few minutes he lets a big gollier go across the floor just missing the men's shoes. MacCarthy is fucking disgusted and he turns around to Duckarse and says 'Dominick, tell that man to stop masticating!' and he walks off with his party. Duckarse looks after him with a real puzzled expression, then he walks over to Ned, clears his throat and says, 'Ned, the boss said you're to take your hand out of your pocket!'"

Jimmy slapped them both on the back and went back to join Milo singing at the conveyor belt. Frankie indicated with his head and, after waiting a moment, Donal slipped out behind him to the jakes. They splashed their way across to the relative quiet of the least flooded of the cubicles and locked the door. "What's the difference between an egg and a wank?" was scrawled in black marker over the corporation-blue paint on the wall. During the third breakdown Frankie had kicked the battered vending machine and rooted up it with a coat-hanger until it yielded up a can of 7-Up as a peace token. "You can't beat a wank!" The words curling down the side of the other wall. Frankie produced the can and a small scrap of silver foil from the pocket of his jeans. He hadn't shaved for a few days and with the light growth of dark hair Donal found it hard to remember that Frankie, at twenty, was only a year older than him.

"Well fuck this for a lark," Frankie said. "Suppose there's no point in asking you for skins, kid?"

"You know me," Donal grinned. "No bad habits."

"There must be a pillow up your mot's dress then. Here, chew on this slowly and then wash it down care of the company. Got it off Tommy on the shift going out. Are you coming to this gig on Friday night or what? Can't you bring Elizabeth with you? Jesus, this jakes is like John Wayne: it's taking shit from nobody."

They watched the turds stirring like goldfish at the rim of the blocked bowl.

"We'd better get back out there," Donal said. "Tell us this, do you think it was the wire or the flux?"

"Who cares. Either way we'll have another breakdown in a minute's time, and just keep on until that wank-that-hatched-out-in-the-sun slows down his machine to the work-to-rule speed."

They resumed their positions as the machine began to rev up and just when it seemed about to start buckling Joe pressed the button and the rapid stream of steel rods began to spit out. Within a minute with the piercing scream of metal on metal the rods stopped and the jammed machine whined hysterically. They could see Duckarse bobbing up and down as he tried to overtake Dan who was steadily wheeling a trolley of empty trays down the path. They walked down the conveyor belt and grabbed Milo by the shoulders.

"Oh macho! Tattoos!" Frankie said pinning the man's shoulders back. "Your arms look like Clery's windows."

"Sure they're nothing at all. A mate of mine had his prick tattooed."

"He did in his bollox," Donal said, keeping one eye on Joe's frantic efforts to restart the machine.

"No, I'm dead serious. Mad Dublin supporter he was. Wanted to show the mots where he came from so he had Dublin done down the side of it."

"Sure it wouldn't bleeding fit for a start."

"Ah, come on. Surely even young lads like you can use your cop-on. Naturally he had to induce a little length into it during the proceedings by thinking about the sister-in-law. Off duty all you could see was the 'D' and 'N' but he assured me that on all state occasions it revealed itself as the true capital of Ireland. Sure I remember being up in a posh hotel in the North of Ireland once and the bloke beside me in the jakes had 'N' and 'Y' tattooed on his."

"Where was he from, Newry?"

"No. Bleeding Newtownmountkennedy!"

"Come on now lads, the machine's running again. Let's make this lost time up."

Duckarse was standing behind them with his hands playing pocket billiards. He stayed there until break time, never saying a word, his eyes just following each load of flux as it came bumping off the raised belt from Frankie's mixer to fall on to the metal tray with the hole for the compressor in front of which Donal stood.

As soon as Donal walked in from the main road past the security hut where the uniformed man sat reading under a single bulb, the first stirrings began in the base of his skull. He walked through the black maze of buildings looming up huge against the night sky until he slipped through the side door into the dried-up air of the factory that reeked of dust and chemicals, with the headache already formed. In the small cloakroom the men sat along wooden benches under the racks of coats and smoked, or else moved around the room like runners testing their fitness before a race. Donal clocked his card in and then went to join them.

"Here's the little daddy-to-be," Jimmy said grinning.

When the hooter cried they moved in groups out towards the machines, eyeing the dockets of the departing shift for any breaches of the work-to-rule. Jimmy and Milo stood at the end of the conveyor belt, banging their empty trays against the frame like overgrown characters from *Oliver*. Frankie wound the lid down over the mixer and the paddles inside consecrated the water and chemicals into flux with a heavy sluggish noise.

"And yes I know how lonely life can be, the shadows follow me, and the wife won't set me free ... " Milo's voice drifted up above the rising sounds of the machines.

After ten minutes Donal's hands worked automatically, brushing the flux down into the hole, hanging on to the handles using all the weight of his body and swinging the slugs across on to the loader as they slowly rose back up out of the compressor. His body adjusted quickly to the pace of work. The worst part was in the mind, whose

13

sole task was to watch the needle rising up to seventy tons and count the number of slugs made. Most of the time he tried to let it go blank and just function as an integral part of the machine, but then minor events from the day would force their way into his thoughts and squat there, refusing to be evicted. For twenty minutes a single remark of Elizabeth or her mother would repeat in his mind until the original meaning was long buried under the bulk of implications that built themselves around it. The breakdowns of the machine provided temporary relief, but also broke the natural rhythm of the body and made it difficult to restart. Above him he could see Frankie taking the piss out of the other team as he danced down past them to reload the hodder in his wrecked jeans that were so dirty the men claimed they walked by themselves when and if he took them off. Behind him he could hear the card machine punching out each minute with a sharp distinct click. Although he tried to ignore it he found his mind waiting for each click until the distance between them seemed to stretch out like a slow water torture against his skull. He had the regular programme of music inside his head, rationed out to last for the whole night. He worked the handles and sang John Prine songs to his machine. The machine never sang back.

At a quarter past three Dan climbed the steep concrete stairs up to the canteen and brewed up two massive urns of tea. He left them on the counter, and taking his own cup from its hiding place in the back of the press, filled it and climbed back down to sit alone with his sandwiches in the cloakroom, his lean tall frame almost buried among the rows of overcoats and donkey jackets. The scab forklift driver parked his truck beside the steel ladder of the storage bay and climbed up to where he now hid his lunch. The men began to congregate around the two cracked basins in the jakes, pushing and slagging and splashing water over each other's hands. The blackened folds of the towel roll had been pulled out until it trailed in a muddy puddle on the floor. Long black imprints of their hands were left over its surface. When the hooter sounded at half past three they climbed up into the canteen to eat their food to the crackle of an all-night pirate radio station. They told blue jokes and stared with open hatred at the forklift driver who shared the bottom table with Joe. Donal sat next to Frankie, sharing in the laughter and trying to control his stomach

14

that was rebelling against the taste of white bread and stale ham. Jimmy was telling them about the war, two brown-stained fingers with a permanent tremor holding a cigarette as he scattered ash all over the tiled floor.

"I went with these two English blokes to this picture house in a little kip of a mountain village in Italy. A bleeding fleapit it was, with a swarm of big insects attracted by the light crawling all over the screen, up the actors' noses and down dresses. The seats were damp and the whole place was in rag order except for this amazing ceiling. It was a really rich blue with these big shiny decorations plastered all over it. Anyway, after a while I gave up trying to follow the picture and just lay back smoking and looking at the ceiling when suddenly this fucking aeroplane flies across it . . . "

Donal turned round and noticed that Frankie had left the room. Immediately he felt insecure in the company, as if he were less a part of the group of men who were all twenty or thirty years older than he. After a moment's unease he washed his cup unnoticed and climbed down the stairs.

From within the cloakroom he could hear Frankie's voice saying, "Ah fuck off with your money, Grandad, it's a present. Sure you can buy me a pint or bring us in a bottle of the duty-free you smuggled home after the Boer War. The driver of the truck from Manchester I was helping unload last week had it in his cabin. I bet you he hasn't even noticed it's gone. They didn't make them like that when you were chasing buffalo across the plains of County Galway during the famine . . . "

Donal hesitated outside the closed door and then walked past to look out the open factory door across the dark encampment of buildings. Outside the night was perfectly still and near freezing point. Off in the distance a car was speeding with a reassuring whine out towards the countryside. He could hear it build up for a gear change before the sound was smothered by the night silence. Kids on a joy-ride probably. Across the yard burning plastic cartons and wooden boxes in the incinerator were thrusting lemon and orange spurts of flame up into the deep blueness of the air. At the edge of the car park an amber spotlight brooded over its charge of vehicles. The total isolation of it all was both frightening and somehow tempting, as if he could just step out under the heavy blue cloak, leaving everything behind him, and he would be swallowed up into the beating heart of that stillness.

He shivered and turned back down the corridor into the cloakroom. He could barely make out the faded blue overalls of Dan pressed back among the coats. Frankie had gone again.

"All alone in the world, Dan?"

"I wouldn't be caught up there with them, with their sick minds and their dirty jokes. Don't be taken in by that shower. They'd tell you jokes with one hand patting you on the shoulder and they'd be taking the eyeballs out of your sockets with the other one."

"Sure they're not that bad at all now, Dan."

The old man held the mug of cold tea to his lips and patted the bench beside him. Donal remained standing before him in the centre of the floor, with his hands uncertainly on his hips. Dan placed the mug back with a resigned air on the chipped surface of the bench. Then he looked up and spoke with that air of sad dignity that both held and repelled the youth.

"Believe me, son, there isn't one of them that for all their crack and their jokes wouldn't leave you lying in the street. Except for your mate Frankie, but even he's half dead already. He isn't the same fellow who came in here a year ago. And he did you no favours when he gave you the tip-off about this place. Listen, you don't belong down here; you're different. You've got brains that you'll never use here. You should be one of those flyboys up in the offices, barrelling around the place from nine to five in a suit. This factory will slowly poison you unless you get out soon. I know what I am talking about . . ."

Duckarse never stepped into the battered room that served as a canteen. At a minute to four he left the foreman's office where he had tea by himself from a flask and kicked the door from the outside, shouting "Time up now, lads!" in a gruff voice, and then, over his shoulder, "Come on!" Donal joined the throng of men as they moved back on to the shop floor. The machines were humming, low and sullen.

The chargehand was now constantly on the watch. Even when the packing line broke down he refused to move away. Down below in the

16

far end of the factory they played cards on the back of one of the unpacked boxes, while the nipper kept a look out for brown coats. Donal sweated under his jumper from the heat of exertion, then froze whenever anybody left the door open behind him. His body had begun to ache and his mind seemed to have been dragged down into a numb gulf of emptiness. The drug Frankie had given him must have been boot polish for its effects had spread through all his limbs, weighing his movements down like mercury. His co-ordination was starting to wander as the endless loads of clay tumbled down on to the tray in front of him like the torrent of water pouring through a childhood memory.

When Donal was six and Frankie seven they built a channel between the two pools they had scooped out in the sloping wilderness of his back garden. In the lower pool they spent days building up a detailed village of muck shops and figures made of stones and mud. Then, having filled the upper pool with kettles of water, Frankie had stepped back and lifted up the lid of the biscuit tin from the channel; they both cheered as the brown water swept down, quickly engulfing the entire model world. Frankie had hurled rocks into it, laughing with the power of a God who could control creation. When Donal looked back there were few childhood memories that did not centre around Frankie. From the moment they met when he was three Donal had quickly fallen into the role of Frankie's lieutenant, the boy Robin to his Batman, the faithful Tonto to his Lone Ranger. And just as easily Frankie had grown into the role of protector, the bodyguard on dangerous and secret missions, the one who stepped in in school yard and street corner with his fists and his boot at the decisive moment. And through all those years they seemed to have only one mind between them. Each day after school they would be together, scheming and planning. And if none of Frankie's schemes ever fully worked out it didn't matter to Donal because there was always a new and even more exciting venture to eclipse the one in progress, and Donal could sit back and be carried on the tide of Frankie's energy. It frightened him now to think back at how close they had been, how they had invented and occupied a secret world together, a world in which they could never have secrets from each other. A day spent without seeing Frankie seemed then like some kind of betrayal. On the few occasions they quarrelled they would find themselves meeting halfway between their houses to make it up. It was the closest thing to love that Donal, lost in the whirlpool of a large family, had ever experienced before meeting Elizabeth.

Then in adolescence they drifted apart without bitterness or even really noticing the change. After he had stepped from that shadow Donal was amazed to discover how much he could do for himself, so that he grew at times almost extrovert in his newly discovered sense of freedom. They had remained friends but the total intimacy had gradually evaporated since that last time they went camping together when Donal was eleven, although neither of them had ever mentioned the event. It all came back to him again now in vivid detail after eight years: the high handlebars of the bicycles glinting in the evening sun, the hill leading past the final houses into the countryside that they freewheeled down and crossing the fields in the growing dusk with the confusion and excitement of pitching the tent. After clowning around and daring each other to run naked to the edge of the field and back, they lay in the blackness, both frightened and thrilled, talking of ghosts and then, inevitably, of women, with their sleeping bags zipped together for warmth. Then after they had stopped speaking for a long time and he was listening to the night sounds in the distance, he felt Frankie's fingers reaching down and gently cupping his balls. Donal waited, passive as ever, erect and pretending to be asleep. He knew that what happened next would be of vital importance. So he just lay there, breathing quietly and trembling a little, and Frankie lay beside him with his hand totally still and gripping. And gradually Donal realised that Frankie didn't know what came next either, and as the older boy withdrew his hand in failure and turned his back both of them realised, although not clearly at first, that their friendship had gone as far as it could go and the only way they could grow was apart.

Donal shuddered now in the cold factory air as he recalled the incident. The door had been left open behind him again and dirt and dried chemicals were blowing in. He watched the next load of flux, wet and loose and unstopable, come towards him up the belt, from Frankie.

Just after half six, when he felt his strength had been fully drained, the huge corrugated skylights above the rusting girders began to lighten in colour, competing with the long flourescent tubes, and he marvelled, as he did every morning, at the hot surge of animal power which took possession of his body. From an unknown source inside him a new strength asserted itself and his spirits began to lift. "Fuck them all!" he sang to the steel face of his machine, "I've got this cunt of a night beaten!"

The first hints of dawn began to spread through the factory and the final hour passed without much effort. At twenty-five past seven the housewives whose children were old enough were standing with their cards in the queue to clock in for the morning. The men washed their hands in the flooded jakes and came in to cluster around them.

"Howya, Jimmy, how's your dick?" one of the girls called.

"Jesus, it's got feathers on it, now you've asked me," the man replied as he charged into them with both hands outstretched. They pushed him back out with shrieks of laughter.

"Get away out of that, ye dirty old man ye. Ye wouldn't even bring us down the pub first and buy us a couple of leg openers!"

Frankie, with his card in one hand and his jacket in the other, grinned at Donal in the crowd as they waited for the hooter to clock out.

They stepped out the small door into the staggering clarity of daybreak. The lawn in front of the offices was glistening, the hedges had hives of patterns from frosted spiderwebs that gleamed in the light. The wooden crates had long ago burned themselves down to ash and only the hint of smoke remained lingering in the air. Their ringing footsteps echoed across the stillness, mixed with the white noise of seagulls circling the wafer-thin film of ice on the back reservoir. Scraps of old newspapers danced rings around their feet. With cigarettes and low mutterings the night shift began tramping out the gates and homeward through the tucked-up streets.

"Tell us, Frankie, how have you managed to stick a year of this place?" Donal asked. "I mean, do you never feel like picking up that shovel of yours and splitting Duckarse or somebody's skull open?"

They were picking their way through the puddles in the muddy back lane they used to take a short cut from the factory grounds. Frankie stopped for a moment to button up the old denim jacket over

19

his sweatshirt and took a cigarette out of his pocket.

"Ah sure, poor old Duckarse is harmless. He's landed with the worst of both worlds. He's no longer one of us and he will never be one of them. Occasionally with someone like MacCarthy you'd be hard pressed to hold yourself back when, say, he's taking one of the new office-girls on a tour of the place and he has his hands all over her in the guise of showing her this or that, and you're working your bollox off with this bloke standing behind you like you were in a freak show. But no matter what you would never lift a finger to him and I'll tell you why. It's nothing to do with morals or any of that shite they fill your head with. If I saw that man lying collapsed on a street corner I'd gladly walk past him. No, it's the fact that they are simply not worth messing your life up for. As it is we're giving them eight hours a day; touch one of them and with our background you'd get sucked into giving them twenty-four hours a day in the Joy or some other jail. Always while you've a bit of hope left you'd never do that unless you were copping out. Listen kid, just keep your head down, bollox up their machines when you can and when you get outside these gates forget about them and enjoy yourself. And have a plan. I'll say mine to you again: Amsterdam or bust. Jesus that time I played the Milky Way. Pubs open till dawn and all the cobbled bridges over the canals and the girls in the windows with the red curtains. And up in Dam Square the blacks in the big leather jackets whispering after you, "Hash, you want hash, man?" and all the barefoot old hippies sitting on the benches with cobwebs hanging out of their beards and a lazy smell of dope off them. I'm just biding me time in this shithole and then I'm making my escape back to civilisation."

The big trucks were thundering in from the countryside, dragging cold shudders of air in their wake as they turned down the Meath Road. In front of them they could see Jimmy arguing, as usual, with his son who worked in the chemical bay. Behind them Dan was walking slowly with Charlie, as old as himself, who over the years had accumulated his own makeshift office among the old storage cases in the packing section. The early commuters were queuing for buses at the bus shelter where the young child's face gazed out from behind the smashed glass of the advertising hoarding.

"Ah well, back to married bliss," Donal said. "How's Barbara keeping?"

"Don't ask me. Sure I never see the mot at all. I climb in beside her at ten to eight when I'm on nights and the next minute her mother is in, banging everything in sight and calling her for work. That woman would live in your ear and make candles from the wax. I used to get more of it before I was married in the long grass of the parish priest's front garden."

"What will you get up to all day so?"

"If this sun keeps up I think it's a day for the magic mushrooms. An old kip will do me till two o'clock, then I'll take a chair out to the garden or open the window of the bedroom and put Dylan on the stereo. Anywhere away from Barbara's family. A couple of mushrooms now will pass the afternoon very nicely till herself comes home. The secret is that you can see anything you like with them. They may be just rows of houses, but one day they're flowers and castles and the next day rows of seats in a rock concert. You can imagine anything you want with them."

They were standing outside the supermarket, wrapped up in the cloying scent of newly baked bread that was coming from the vents in the wall. At the entrance a man in an old army overcoat sold newspapers with his fingers sticking from the sawn-off tops of woollen gloves.

"Then what?"

"She comes home. Makes me dinner. We play a few records or go down and watch the box with her mother burning holes in the back of me neck. Then I bale out to meet the lads in the band for a pint and a few joints and wind up at half eleven doing my French chef impersonation on the mixer. I tell you, get a place of your own, Donal, somewhere where you can make a stand. You'll fall into the same trap as I did. That hatchet-faced serpent is creaming me off for just one room. Jesus she'd sell a rat's hole to a blind man for a wedding ring. Barbara's mother never heard of the work-to-rule. Listen, I'm off for me five minute snuggle. Don't forget the gig on Saturday night. And bring Elizabeth. Cheers."

The stream of schoolchildren veered around him as if he didn't exist as Donal walked home to bed through the rising streets. He

21

moved against the flow of people like a fish struggling up-river out of season.

Two

HE TURNED the front key gently in the lock and listened for a moment before tiptoeing down the hall, breathing in the smell of floor polish and the stale reminder of cooking, across the shining tiles in the kitchen and out again into the privacy of the back garden. The early light seemed to hover over the garden with a tactile clarity, focused in long rays through the branches of the trees and lighting up the grass like the rich touched-up colours of a film. Donal's shoes slipped on the dew of the wild lawn as he tried to avoid crunching over the freshly-laid gravel path. The caravan stood in the bottom corner of the garden with a thick overgrown hedge spilling out from the back of it and a lilac tree overshadowing the roof on one side. In the hedge a single bird was testing the airwaves. The first lilac buds were starting to blister the pale bark along the slender branches. Just ten months ago he remembered picking a vast bunch for her as she stood below him in her school uniform catching the stems excitedly. Lilac was short-lived, a firework caught in a branch that burned up in slow motion.

He turned the handle of the door and stepped quietly inside. The light straining through the tinted skylight was fern-coloured. It nestled in a green frame around her head on the pillow as she slept with her limbs tucked up into a ball. Her fair hair was tousled over her eyes and her face so relaxed and abandoned in sleep that she could easily pass for sixteen, her age when they had first met in the swirling heat of a dancehall two years before. In the fragile light of early morning it seemed impossible that such a childlike frame could itself have been carrying his child for nearly four months.

Perhaps it was all a dream. There was choking in his throat as he watched her which he knew was love. It burned inside of him, as physical a sensation as exhaustion or hunger, and yet a different, insatiable feeling that gnawed within like a growth he could do nothing to control. She was so china-doll-like as he stood there dirty and tired that he watched over her with a sense, almost, of awe.

If she was awake when he came in Donal scolded her, yet when she slept on like this, without acknowledging his presence, he always felt a sense of disappointment and, unaccountably, a tremor of unease, as if he were an intruder who had stumbled upon an intimate and private scene. Six weeks of marriage had not adjusted him to the tiny insignificant moments of shared life. All around him in the caravan were the possessions they had begun to accumulate on expeditions to the shopping centre together, which Donal dreaded. He knew his presence was not needed, but that Elizabeth wanted him to share in every purchase as if each of them were indirectly a bond bringing them closer together. So he moved among the pots and the tea sets, the sheets and the basins on Saturday afternoons when he would normally have been playing football or enjoying an extended lie-on after the week. But behind his slightly embarrassed impatience on these trips he was proud of the small world they had built up in such a short space of time, the few possessions that were to be the foundations for a life thrust upon them.

He undressed and folded a blanket over the window to dull the light before pulling back the sheets. She was wearing her light white nightdress, rumpled up over her legs. He lay down beside her in the warmth of the sheets, feeling the softness of her skin against his like ointment on a wound. Still she didn't wake, although her hot body stirred, protesting at the intrusion of cold flesh, and she half turned over on to her front, drawing the bedclothes back towards her. He lay clumsily against her back, watching each breath form and break within her rising shoulders. Four months ago the idea of being able to share a bed openly with her without her two married brothers chasing him around Dublin with shotguns would have appeared both wonderful and impossible. As it was, looking back, he had probably been lucky to escape with his life. He was finding that if he desired something strongly enough he normally got it, but never in the way he had imagined or planned. On some mornings the door of the caravan

24

closed behind him like a coffin lid, confining his life to this small space just when he had begun to realise the scope of it. For eight hours, through darkness into dawn, he had sweated so her turned back could fall and rise through dreams. Exhaustion suddenly made him bitter and disappointed. He could manage without anyone. He was completely alone.

The rush of cold air woke him. He reached out, clutching at space, as if a part of his body he had only been dimly aware of had been torn from him without warning. His lips formed her name in the headlong panic of waking. He could see the back of her fair hair as she leaned over the side of the narrow mattress being sick as quietly as possible. His anger was gone, replaced by a jaded and helpless concern. Needing some role to frame his emotions lest he break down, he held her shoulders, squeezing them softly until she leaned her head back against him. She turned and quickly burrowed her body against his and kissed his naked shoulder. He held her tightly in his arms and gazed up at the discoloured clouds through the skylight. Then he ran his fingers along her back, crumpling her nightdress smoothly down, and said, "Lie back, I'll make you some tea."

She snuggled more tightly against him and whispered, "It came over me so suddenly I couldn't even get out of bed. You should have woken me, Donal. You know I always want to be awake when you come in from that place. I missed you; don't move, Donal, just hold me please."

* * * * * *

Dan got off the bus at Crossgun's Bridge and, crossing the railway bridge, turned down the beaten grass of the canal bank. The water built up into a calm solid off-white sheet that edged its way towards the lock where it was wrung out into a whitish spray over the wreck of the car trapped below. The two swans lifted their tall necks from the reeds on the far side and began to zig-zag across the surface towards the old man, appearing awkward and less graceful when he saw them close up. They snatched up the remains of his sandwiches, refusing to come too near the path, and when they were certain nothing was left, turned their backs dismissively and paddled back among the sodden reeds. Dan moved back up the path and out again into the chaos of the early rush-hour traffic and the crowds pushing past him scurrying to work.

The small handwritten envelope with the English postmark was lying in the hall for him amid the confetti of bills and circulars for tenants who had long since absconded with rent owing. He carried it upstairs and left it on the mantelpiece behind the heavy old-fashioned clock until Saturday night. He reached deep into his coat pocket and produced the paper bag that Frankie had given him. He stared at it for a moment as if tempted to examine the contents, then, with a sigh, placed it under the mattress. The room was cold on account of the window he had left open to try and rid it of the damp smell that always built up inside the place. He stood on the shaky chair to put fifty pence in the meter and then placed the kettle on one of the two rings on the small cooker that stood on the work-top beside the sink. He never felt at ease until he had taken care of the rent, so he counted it into a small envelope and carried it downstairs with a note about the cracked pane of glass in the toilet which he knew would be ignored. The note was a ploy so that the landlord would avoid calling for fear he might be forced to do repairs. Working nights at least had the advantage of Dan's being able to fake sleep if he did call. Dan only saw him occasionally, a stout porter-faced man, often still in his garda sergeant's uniform, peering around at the condition of the room as he collected the week's rent and fending off all questions about the state of the house with a professional "huh!"

The kettle was beginning to hum on the blue flame when he went back to the room. He bolted the door and leaned against it for a moment with his eyes shut. Then, after filling a mug with a teabag in it almost to the brim, he took an egg from the small press and placed it inside the boiling kettle with a twist of salt. He took his black shoes off and stretched himself out on top of the bed. His eyes were stiff from lack of sleep. With any luck the young fellow upstairs on the dole would have been out all night and wouldn't be tramping about and playing music until after midday. He would never get away with it when Dan first moved into digs, but the only thing that had remained

26

the same since then was the cheap furniture. Nobody cared anymore. This morning on the bus two schoolboys had hurled a seat down the stairs, laughing at the top of their voices. Nobody looked up from their newspapers. They might not have existed.

He should get up and take the egg off the gas, but he just wanted to lie here and sleep. That boy in work upset him. So many of them he had seen come in over the years blossoming into life and then slowly freezing up like plants left out to wither in a winter field. Give him another year and every inch of humanity would be squeezed out of him. As soon as this work-to-rule was forgotten about they would be back working flat-out trying to make bonus money, intent on passing their quota and nothing else. They would quickly get used to the extra money until the inhuman pace became the norm and they burnt themselves out. Already the older lad Frankie was gone, although he still didn't know it himself. Dan had nobody else to care for, he reasoned, so why shouldn't he care for them? To sit there in that cold cloakroom, night after night, hoping that one of them would come down, and then when the young fellow did all he could do was scold him when there was so much that he would lie here in this room rehearsing to tell him. But even that, just to talk to one of them for a few moments, gave the night warmth and made it bearable.

He stood up carefully and knocked the ring off. The teabag floated on the rim of the mug like a bloated carcass. He turned to where, above the bed, the chipped blue statue of the young woman looked down over him with a shy concerned smile. From habit he knelt, but it was years since he had been able to repeat the old formula of words. He buried his head in his hands against the mattress and tried to think. Hail Mary, for sixty years I've knelt before you, and though my world has changed beyond all recognition my devotion to you remains true. Another dawn, Mary, another step down that tunnel. Each morning I feel that I cannot go on alone. I cannot live with this sourness, with this emptiness. How much further do I need to go to prove myself to you? Everything I taste now is bitter. Just one sign is all I ask. I need to have tasted your freshness just once. Mary, let your eyes show me that all these years have not been for nothing.

Through the walls he could hear the sharp hissing of half-frozen taps. He lay on top of the bed knowing that at least his exhaustion

27

would bring sleep quickly. As he closed his eyes the cold spring sunlight filtered through the tiny holes in the lace curtain, which rocked faintly in the breeze, casting thin worms of warm light that played across his face.

* * * * * *

Donal was back in his old house waiting for an important letter, the results of an exam or interview, something that would change his entire life. He had left his bedroom and was standing on the cold landing in his bare feet, leaning over the banister to look down. Through the distorted glass above the front door he recognised the blurred shape of the postman approaching. He waited in nervous anticipation for the letter to fall through the slot, ready to race down the stairs. Instead the door slowly swung open by itself. A short, thin countryman in his sixties stood on the doorstep gazing down the hall. Donal followed his gaze. Directly below him, in the kitchen doorway, a middle-aged woman in a blue hat was silently waiting. Without looking up she began to walk towards the man. Against his will Donal felt his feet begin to draw him down the stairs as the old couple walked towards the gate. They stopped and turned in silence, staring back at him in the doorway as if he were an intruder into their lives. Who were these strangers invading his house? Why didn't they speak, move or do something, anything instead of that stare full of accusation and resentment. He could feel the hair on the back of his neck begin to stiffen and his limbs rise. Then with a sudden jerk of his entire body he snapped awake.

"How long have you been sitting there?" he asked.

"Only a little while. You seemed to be sleeping so peacefully."

"I wasn't, I was . . . never mind. What time is it?"

He reached out his hand to take Elizabeth's as she sat at the end of the bed in the slanting light of late afternoon. There was a feeling of nausea at the bottom of his stomach and his eyes were screwed up and sore from the light. She took his hand and cupped it between her palms. Since he started to work shifts his stomach had begun to trouble him. It was like a faint pins and needles constantly in the lining and a heavy sluggishness as if something were swilling around inside of him. Just when the metabolism had begun to adjust to having lunch at half three at night he was switched to mornings and then, in turn, to evenings. With his free hand he wiped the scum of sleep from his mouth and smiled.

"It's just after four," Elizabeth said. "Mammy says you're to come up to the house for a bite to eat."

"Tell her I'm still asleep."

"Liar! She's not after your body or anything you know. She's going to think it's strange if we're always hiding down here like we were ashamed or something."

"No, it's not that. I'm just still half asleep. Oi, slip in here beside me and we'll see what pops up!"

Elizabeth giggled and lifted the blanket over the window to look up at the house before kicking off her shoes and slipping in between the sheets.

"But only for a few minutes. Oh Jesus you're all warm!"

Once they had grasped at any such opportunity, sneaking out into gardens at parties or hiding themselves under the black shadows in the littered secrecy beneath the metal bridge. But now that he had all the time and permission of the world he no longer seemed certain of when was the right time. Through her tee-shirt he could feel her breasts pressing against him. Were the nipples hardening? How little he knew, he was discovering, of aspects of Elizabeth's personality. Released from the threat of pregnancy at times her behaviour surprised and, for some reason, even shocked him. She had always been the passive partner; now she could play with and tease him, learning quickly and anxious to experiment with the full range of positions. And yet again in the daylight she was innocent and childish, going off into giggles and uncontrollable blushing as she neared the punchline of a blue joke. He reached his hand in under her tee-shirt.

A ball was kicked down the garden towards the caravan and they heard her mother shout: "Johnny! Get that ball out of there at once. Bring it out and play on the road."

Elizabeth sighed and squeezed him before pulling the sheet back.

"Come on Tarzan, we'd better put in appearance before Jane's

29

mother eats all the Snake and Pygmy pie."

"Tell her I'll be up in five minutes. I want to have a wash. You stroll on up and keep the peace."

She slipped her shoes back on, wiggled the backside of her jeans and blew him a kiss, grinning over her shoulder as she left. He lay down again among the rumpled sheets. That little kid used to hero-worship him when he was calling to take Elizabeth out. He had shown him how to head the ball properly and how to kick with the left foot. In return he had enjoyed living out the enlarged image of himself. Johnny had even been excited when he had learned that Donal was coming to live in the back garden. It was Mrs Kelly who expelled him.

"He needs his rest. Sure the young fellow is working for a place of his own."

Donal could hear the grating politer tones imposed over the natural music of the woman's Cavan accent. The boy blamed him. He could sense it in the sullen silence whenever they met. Ten year olds don't lie. They know why their world is upset.

He rose from the bed and switched the electric heater on, then poured water into the basin and, slipping off his underpants, stood naked before the mirror. Already last night seemed like days before. It came back to him with a dull unreal glow, a single collage of so many emotions: humour and exhaustion, play-acting and depression. The only memory that stood out in his mind was the rake-like figure of Dan hovering over the cloakroom like a conscience. He knew that what the old man said was right, but with each passing week it became more difficult to retain the enthusiasm for job hunting. Especially over the last few nightmare months. Still, he knew that he must make time for it and for all the other unfinished business that was hanging around his neck.

It was half past four on the clock beside the basin. Girls who had just been released from school were now walking home in packs, planning their Friday night as they exchanged blouses and dates. In offices and factories young men were discreetly checking the clock, hoping the traffic wouldn't be too clogged up or that the ex-Special Branch bouncer wasn't on the door of the dancehall tonight. The day shift would have clocked out at half three. They'd be sitting at home now watching Playschool on the box after their dinner, or settling into their third pint in the Bottom of the Hill, the laughter rising over the quiet thud of darts above their heads, the whispering chalk on the discoloured blackboard, the automatic arithmetic of doubles and trebles. All over the city a weekend mood would be starting to settle like a vapour. He had a date to keep with a slugger in seven hours time.

With the window still blocked by the blanket the only light came through the glass over the door and the coloured skylight above his head. He stood naked, drying himself in the centre of that fading shaft of jade light. It was like standing at the bottom of an invisible pit he had woken in. As yet he still didn't know how to begin to scale its transparent heights. And yet despite all his unease he felt about the caravan as he had never felt for any other place. Although it was tiny and only on loan, squatting out in the back of another person's garden, for the first time in his life he felt himself to be at home in his own place. A part of him he had never understood before asserted itself once inside these walls. He could lie on the bed here and feel free of everyone except the one person he wanted to be with. Although he had shared a room with two brothers all his life it has been no preparation for this experience of actually living with a person. Rising with her, worrying about her, trying to surrender a part of yourself to her without knowing how much to give and what to hold back. Making decisions for her.

Up to now there had never been any real pressure on him to make decisions. Water had been poured on his head, school carefully mapped out. His parents even seemed to have little choice in the matter. He had been fitted with suits and rosettes and propelled towards some unspecified role in the future. Even the job he had finally landed had been beyond his control. Maybe once there had been a choice, but already he had spent seven months growing stupid on the labour. Most of his classmates were still engaged in the daily ritual of the marathon card-session on the green in front of the houses, taking an odd stolen car for a spin and splashing their dole money on one good night each week. Life changing gear and taking off for a few hours. Six or seven pints in the Metro or the Blue Lion, a gig with a hungry raw band in the Ivy Rooms and maybe an attempt to crash a disco in jeans or parallels. On Saturday night large flagons of cider passed from hand to hand around the fire in the few fields left among the mushrooming estates. The seats from dumped cars spread out in a circle to sit on. The young mots of thirteen or fourteen sneaking over from the knackers' caravans looking for a swig. "Mister I'll climb in beside you, so I will." Hoping for a chase home to the camp across the dangerous blackness of the fields. "Jesus, Maria, pull him off me!" Three or four of them closing in with boots and shrieks and the smell of unwashed flesh if one of them was caught.

Even the one decision he had taken he was uncertain of – that night when Elizabeth couldn't tell him what was wrong; scribbling shapes and crazy designs over the newspaper on her knee with her eyes down until he finally asked her straight out, and she nodded without looking up, once, then twice after a long pause. That night in January when he had stared across the sofa in numb shock, saying to himself "God no! No, it couldn't be me!"; when he didn't know whether to take her in his arms or to run. She had finally looked up and her eyes were dry and watching him. He put his arm around her and they went walking like strangers for hours through the moonlit streets, with her head leaning against his shoulder and her faith in him alone carrying her. They had stopped by the ivy-covered factory wall where the final street lights vanished down a country road, and against the vast black presence of the fields he bent down and kissed her.

"Elizabeth, let's get married. We would have one day anyway when the money was there."

"You don't have to, Donal." She paused and he could hear the uncertainty in her voice muffled by his jacket. "I could manage. I could."

"I want to. Christ, how I love you. I wanted to all along you know."

The right decision. The choice left in his hands and firmly taken. Inside he felt his heart pounding, the blood throbbing rapidly against his skull. Very far away he could hear the calmness of his voice. He prayed she didn't notice his trembling. All the way home his jokes and their laughter and then the tears shared in the kitchen as their emotions spilt over. Elizabeth on his knee, hugging him as they swayed back and forth under the bright arc of the electric light bulb,

32

with both of them realising that they had known it would happen like this. And even now, three months later, although in a moment she would bounce back through the door with her whole face electrified and blushing with life and laughter, he could still sense how frightened she was in those unconscious moments when he caught her retreating inside her own mind or when he woke to find her body shivering in a nightmare beside his. Why had the reasons for the decision begun to haunt him? He gazed at the small mirror beside the sink and asked himself for the thousandth time, had he done it because he loved her or because he was conditioned to from birth? The thread of his life mapped out and he automatically being drawn on by it? Did he need to keep the illusion that he was still in control inside his mind? And had it even been taken on that night in Dublin, or had he, or she, taken it in that hotel those weeks beforehand, unconsciously forcing their worst fears to happen, bringing their nightmares out to dwell in the light and grow flesh and blood and away from ever disturbing their sleep again?

"Come on out of that. De Valera had a shorter lying-in-state than you've had. Is this a strip show is it?"

Her face burst in through the door, playful again. She moved around him, her hands distracting him in every way possible as he tried to put his clothes on, until they both wound up laughing, lying back among the rumpled sheets again.

* * * * * *

People passing the statue on their way from work would see Dan there on the evenings when he worked night shift. Once, when children queued for hours down the side of the cinema beside the park, the statue had held a rifle. Now the cinema was closed down and the bronze volunteer knelt in his republican uniform, guarding over the park with both hands chopped off. Two benches down the narrow strip of grass Dan sat with his hands buried deeply in his overcoat pockets and his eyes resting on the statue. There were a few of the usual clientele dealt out on to the benches around him. The small old

33

man to Dan's left always came late in the evenings and, having peered carefully around him, produced from inside his torn overcoat a pile of children's comics. He hunched his shoulders over the thin pages, reading them intently with a wide, absorbed grin across his face. The woman he knew as Bríd sat on the next seat with her sack of belongings balanced between her two boots. In every weather she was wrapped in her selection of discarded overcoats. Her face had a squashed look as if some part of it had slowly been eroded with wear over the years. Dan could see her having a mumbled conversation with herself or some imaginary listener. The young man who had been coming here since the evening he told Dan he was made redundant sat with the shellshocked look he constantly wore. There was still a restlessness and possibly a hope within him that meant he was not yet fully invested within the company.

Dan had grown to consider them in his mind as a single group whose sole qualification for membership was to belong nowhere else and to have ceased trying to fit in anywhere else. Somehow he never considered himself as part of the company. Most days they left each other to sit in peace, maybe pausing for a moment on their way out, like the white-haired man who sat in the walled garden at the end and said every evening to him, "The one thing that will kill you for sure is stress," before walking slowly down the path. For Dan, perpetually torn between the need for anonymity and the old longing for company, it was as good a compromise as he could achieve. Occasionally he was approached for longer because he could listen without commiting the mortal sin of giving advice or attempting to unburden himself in turn. By now he was able to piece together the lives of those around him: lives that had begun normally enough, but each of which was like an engine with a grain of dust inside that would one day clog up the machine. They, in their turn, seemed too absorbed in their private maladies to be inquisitive as to how he came to pass his time among their ranks.

A few winos who used the park knew he was a soft touch for a few bob, but only if touched indirectly. At the direct approach, the dirt-brown hand held out and the mumbled words with the pleading look, he would stare them out or reply with a curt "No." The method was to sit down quietly on the same bench and give him a few minutes to soften up and become so aware of their presence that breaking the silence became a blessing after the tortuous build-up. After that it was easy to bring the conversation around to food or how cold it was when sleeping out at night. The hook sank in quickly and soon the hand was drawn across. "Get a few chips," he'd say, or "Go over to the Ivy Hostel tonight. Sure at least you'll be warm." Then as soon as they began their thanks he was gone, a tall lean figure who never looked back, as if embarrassed by the scene that had just taken place.

The nearest people to him tonight were two youngsters in gleaming FCA uniforms. He could hear the tallest of them talking, their cigarette tips reddening in the gloom. Dan watched the fair-haired lad with the ginger rumour of a moustache over his lip and the scars of the slow battle against acne still racing across his face.

"It makes you feel that you're really somebody," he was saying. "Like last weekend I was guarding this bridge on a manoeuvre in Athlone and, you should have seen the people passing look at me. I mean they didn't know the gun wasn't loaded. I know it's great crack with the gargle, and the mots, and that, but I mean you really feel you're somebody as well."

Dan looked up at the proud uniform of the statue squatting like a sniper on the pillar in the deepening twilight as the two lads made their way off to drill with old World War I rifles. He thought to himself that there were no statues of how those who didn't make the corridors of power looked twenty years after the truce, squabbling over details of inflated attacks in pubs where they became vague tourist attractions, or staring out from dead-end jobs over a stagnant Free State which had no use for them except to parade at an ever increasing number of funerals. Or else trying to break into big-time crime in the States like Dan Breen, or still racketeering like Barney Flaherty back home. Ignored by the history books for his delight in murder. Still vanishing from the village for weeks on end when Dan used to go home in the fifties, and cycling twice a week to meet a girl young enough to be his grand-daughter. When she became pregnant Flaherty abandoned her and continued to live in the village without a word spoken against him. The girl's mother left the child on his doorstep after it was born and he thundered down to the barracks with it.

"Take the little bastard back," he shouted, pressing the young guard up against the wall. That child probably had children of his own now and people would still be afraid to tell him who his father was. Barney Flaherty had made the fatal mistake of not dying. Like Ernie O'Malley, there were no statues to him.

This narrow strip of park had once been a stretch of the Royal Canal, branching out near the grey bulk of Mountjoy Jail and flowing down to the Broadstone. Its stagnant water had been considered redundant and was laid to rest with earth and flowers. Now with nightfall the dispossessed were beginning to climb the steps out of the hollow like mourners who had gathered around the tomb of lives that had outlived their purpose. Most of them would be lucky if as many gathered when they too finally stepped out from life. He was alone now among the shrubs and the bones of the benches.

So many parks he had sat in throughout his life and for so many reasons. A lifetime spent sitting in public places, dreading company and yet aching for somebody to talk to. The tongue-tiedness of being incapable of approaching another person that he hid under the pensive pose. A man that people might think had some dark secret to brood on, who had no past worth remembering. When he had first arrived in Dublin in 1934 he had sat in St Stephen's Green with Patricia after their Legion of Mary meetings. Her curling black hair and her laughter at his nineteen-year-old stammer came back to him too distant to hurt any longer. Those long awkward pauses when he was unable to repeat the words that, looking back, he only needed to say. Always the image of her he had invented in a thousand rehearsed scenes in his digs at night would come between him and the reality. He remembered her hand warm in his, teasing him, as she distributed the little tracts on purity and the Virgin. And her flirting jokes with the middle-aged dandies turned out immaculately by their landladies every Tuesday evening. After her wedding, a shotgun affair at twenty to a lay brother in the ward, he used to sit alone in their enclosed seat beside the pond and try to understand what he had allowed to slip away from him.

The rosebeds and the fountain were a long way from the overgrown park beside the Protestant church when he used to go to town once a week as a child. One night after the parish dance he had watched a man and woman climb the railings and vanish into the undergrowth. He remembered how the man had hung his cap on a spike and the woman had hitched her skirts up and stepped on to the man's joined hands and when she was half over she turned and saw him and laughed, and the man had shouted at him to go away. And he had stood there after they disappeared, knowing that a different world lay somewhere within that dark cluster of trees, and with a shiver realised that something was happening to his body he had never experienced before.

After the war in London he had no choice but to sit in that small park near Holborn to avoid the tall willowy girl in her early thirties who kept calling to his digs. They had met at one of the few dances he had found the courage to go to and he discovered himself released from his shyness by a babble of stage-Irish chatter. And afterwards, astonished at how easy it was, he had found himself back in her small bed-sit, saying crazy things, anything to experience the lipsticked lips where her tongue kept getting in the way and to feel the hardened folds of her lacquered hair. Then she pulled him back on to her bed, repeating over and over, "Say you don't think I'm a tart. Say you don't!" and a virgin at thirty-one he had entered her and panicked, floundering like a lunatic until he came with a spent, incomplete feeling that hurt all the way home.

He never managed to forget her plain nice face with its slightly protruding teeth and the wide upward look of her eyes as if inviting hurt. He went back four times in the next two weeks, each time hating himself more as the lies repeated themselves. The greatest shock had not been in the discovery that the physical contact could not match his fevered imaginings, but in finding a person more desperate than himself, who was willing to risk everything in the terror of oncoming spinsterhood. Then he stopped calling and tried to break loose and the price, as usual, had to be paid. He sent her notes, trying not to hurt her feelings, and invented stories that rebounded on him, growing more and more complex with each telling. Finally he just sat in the park on those late summer evenings rather than face a confrontation until she stopped calling. Often in the past he had felt himself in love with a girl and knew the rituals so well; the lonely vigils and the drawn-out walks past the places associated with her. But to find himself the beloved, with the reponsibility of another life thrust upon him, was worse, and the actions he once repeated so often seemed absurd and humiliating in another.

She was found with an overdose of tablets and kept overnight in hospital. He had called then to her flat and she had screamed at him and called him an Irish bastard, and the landlady's little dog had been woken by the noise and ran snapping at him as he found himself walking, perfectly calm, down the hall with the landlady's husband standing in the kitchen doorway staring at him. And as he walked down the driveway under the streetlight outside he felt a weight lift from his shoulders as she screamed abuse after him, as if her taunts and insults freed him from the recent past.

He turned the collar of his overcoat up and rose from the bench. These days he just sat here because he had nothing better to do and it was a way of getting out of his flat that was still private. The evening rush-hour was dying down at the traffic lights. The Hut pub was doing its normal Friday evening trade. He would get an *Evening Herald* at the shop beside the hospital. An evening with the paper and the wild west of Zane Grey, the music from the stereo upstairs and maybe one of the girls below calling in for sugar or something. A rest for an hour or two and then that desperado in the factory rounding up his posse and trying for an all-out strike to add another notch to his pistol. Zane Grey would have had him shot by page fifty.

He paused outside the Mater Hospital to watch the men with grey faces and newspapers under their arms steal out the back entrance from the weekly VD clinic. They came quietly from the out-patients department where, up two unsignposted flights of stairs, they had sat in long silent rows on benches, waiting for their numbers to be called. Dan could never tell by their faces whose results were negative and whose positive. Over the years he had learned to make out the lucky ones by the crumpled pieces of paper with their numbers on it which they dropped on the pavement like pieces of their lives as they slipped quietly into the evening darkness.

Three

LOOK, LADS, the issues at stake here are pure and simple. MacCarthy must be made to give into us this time or we can never hope to be in a good bargaining position again. They know we have them over a barrel because of this New Zealand order. They will never be able to fill it on schedule without overtime."

"We can't fill our stomachs with bonus and overtime either." The mutterings began from the men again and the room seemed about to dissolve into a dozen minor meetings.

Toby stopped pacing back and forth with one hand holding the lapel of his jacket and quietened the men by raising his palm.

"Listen now, we've got to follow through our support of the girls and protect the manning levels. They've tried to make the women work night shift since they got equal pay. Now, firstly, the girls can't do that because they are not able to be away from their children at night. Secondly, there are already men paid to work permanent nights as checkers. What will happen is that those women with young kids would have to leave if they are forced to work nights and the men night checkers who leave or retire will not be replaced. And that means that management can run down the workforce by fifteen or twenty jobs without having to pay a single penny in redundancy money. And once they go who knows what jobs will be next?"

"Okay, we know that bit. That's all clear," Jimmy said from the table beside Donal. "But what's worrying me is where is this dispute leading? I've never backed down from a strike yet and I've been in a quare few, but I'd like to know where I'm going. I mean, when MacCarthy tried to impose the new conditions on the girls we staged a one-day strike and he chickened out before lunch time. All was rosy

39

in the garden again."

"He agreed to postpone the new rosters pending further negotiations," Toby corrected him.

"Yes, well around here that's always meant that the whole yoke has been forgotten about."

"Well, fair enough – although you're only fooling yourself if you think he will give in that easy. We would have let it rest there too, for the moment, if it hadn't been for them getting that scab to unload the truck from London with his forklift, earning bonus while the rest of us were sitting up in that canteen losing half a day's pay. Now we agreed up there, didn't we," Toby looked around the room as if inviting contradiction, "that the unloaded wire was blacked?" A murmer of agreement rose from the men. "And we are still refusing to run it through the machines until we are compensated for our loss of earnings for that morning and, more importantly, while we can use the wire as a bargaining tool, until we get firm guarantees that the status quo is retained for the women and we don't find ourselves back to square one again. Three weeks ago they tried to take disciplinary action when they brought the wire down to B machine and the crew wouldn't touch it, and so we used our legitimate right to work-to-rule in retaliation. If we are going to back down now then our position in any future dispute is hopeless. Every one of us here voted for the action, didn't we . . . ?"

Toby had only been in the factory three months longer than Donal but was already in command when he arrived just before Christmas. The men respected him as a hard-working shop steward who would work in their interests but Donal suspected that they had never grown to trust him fully as an intermediary between MacCarthy and themselves. Yet at the same time nobody else in the factory had as good an understanding of the minefield of industrial relations or was eager to venture into a dispute that grew more cloudy as it progressed.

They sat on the battered chairs and chipped table tops in the canteen, or leaned against the walls smoking. Already they had lost half an hour's pay listening to Toby speak, Donal thought. With the full night shift and a dozen of the evening shift who had stayed to hear him he had a difficult audience to contend with, but he still managed to hold the meeting together above the confused babble of voices.

40

One could tell the lads from the chemical bay by the coating of fine powder and dust that discoloured their overalls. Jimmy's son was among them, grinning at his father who was trying to make a point over the raised voices. The staff of the packing line huddled together around the corner table in much the same way as they spent their time in the dingy alcove at the rear of the factory. The two crews of the production lines mixed freely in the centre of the room, exchanging jokes with one another in low voices. Down below in the cloakroom Dan waited, refusing to scab and being docked like the rest of them, but taking no part in the proceedings. And in the brightly lit emptiness of the shop floor an engine raised its metallic growl over the humming of the waiting machines, a forklift putted to a halt and a man climbed the rusting steel ladder to the high platform where he hid his tools and personal belongings.

One or two of them had come by car, a number on bicycles, but most came on foot down the black lanes that skirted the factories, past the works fountain in the front reservoir splashing white snakes of water out into the night, and on towards the wooden door that opened in the black factory wall every few minutes like a match flaring in the darkness. The footsteps quickened as half eleven drew nearer until the hooter gave three slow black moans across the empty sky and they slackened again. Why bother hurrying when a quarter of an hour's pay has already been docked?

Donal had met Frankie for a pint at ten o'clock in the pub in the village where the normal Friday night singalong was in full swing.

"Well kid, four months in the job," Frankie said. "I thought you were only passing through until you got fixed up elsewhere?"

"Ah, I'm starting to think I'll be here for life. Sure I haven't the energy to go looking for other jobs. It's been a crazy few months, you know."

"Wasn't I through it. Keep your John Thomas in your pocket or you're fucked, if you'll forgive the pun. Even John Lennon's was a shotgun job the first time."

The two old men at the table behind were singing "I Did It My Way" in different keys.

"I don't know why I married you, you old bastard," a stout-breasted woman roared across at the most wizened of them.

41

"Go away, Maggie, you're drunk," he said, raising his hand to block her fist and pushing her away.

"Hit the defenceless women, would ye?" the few women watching joined in.

The extractor fan in the ceiling was too weak to lift the veil of smoke but added a loud crackle to the din of voices and glasses every few seconds. Frankie pushed his way into the bar and brought two white-collared black pints expertly back over an ocean of bobbing heads. He tasted his with a sip and placed it down on the flooded surface of the table. He wiped the white cream from his lip and settled back.

"Do you know what, Donal?" he said. "Having a conversation up in that place is like trying to wangle a ride in a convent. Go into the jakes there and meet one of the lads and you can talk to them about the sun, moon and stars. But wait till you get two of the younger ones together. They strut around the place, each terrified of betraying signs of intelligence to the other. They are like those CB headers, all tuning down to the one wavelength to conduct their conversations. Like last night when I got that dope off Tommy on the other shift. I was there having a fag before clocking in and he was changing to go out and we were talking about music and, naturally, about God himself, Bob Dylan. I asked him if he had 'Blood on the Tracks' and he said, 'Yeah, great bleeding album,' and then I said to him, 'Do you know that track, "Come in, she said, I'll give you shelter from the storm"? I think that's about trying to get back into the womb out of all the hassle of life.' Fuck sake, you'd swear I'd just been found touching up his granny. 'What do you mean it's about?' he says. 'It's not about bleeding anything. It's just a fucking song. Right!' And then he storms off to clock out."

"Ah, Tommy probably thinks about things in his own way." Donal could see that Frankie was growing more serious as he progressed through the pint. It was a side of him he remembered well from childhood but which he had rarely seen since starting in the factory. It seemed as if a haze lifted momentarily from a mountain which one had grown accustomed to regarding as soft and revealed the hard stones underneath.

"No, the whole point of the operation is not to think about anything,

42

to go through life not being responsible for your actions. That's what these boys are into. I'll tell you about a dream I've been having since I started working there. At the beginning I'm standing in total pitch blackness, not knowing where I am, with this faint crying in the distance and then, very faintly, I hear the noise of waves and, surprisingly close, I can see the white flashes of foam breaking. And all the time the wailing is getting stronger and more piercing. At first I think it's sea birds but it's too human like. Then I take a few steps and I fall over something huge and wet and blubbery and it lets out a soft little gasp and rolls over as the light begins to break and I find myself staring down at this fifteen-foot whale, unable to breath and gazing up at me all big eyes and blubber. It's strange, I think they're much bigger in real life. But now the light is really clear and cold and I can see down miles of beach covered with shoals of these ugly grey whales that have hauled themselves out of the water to die of suffocation. One of them must have been beached and the rest followed his cries. There's hundreds of them and they're piled three and four deep in places, smeared with wet sand and crying with their sides heaving as they wait to die. And in the centre of it all I'm standing by myself with my hair frozen stiff with terror and then I just wake up with a shudder covered in sweat. I know who those fucking whales are, Donal. They are you and me and Tommy and the rest of us sweating our balls off by day and then going out and blowing every chance we ever have of making it. We're all frantic to burn ourselves out like racing drivers who've spun off the track and can only sit there as noble failures with the outcome of the race beyond their control."

Donal watched Frankie's eyes as they surveyed the mayhem taking place in all corners of the packed pub.

"Bedad it must be some quare stuff you're taking," he joked.

Frankie suddenly grinned as if relieved at the escape route out of the conversation and grabbed Donal's knee, saying, "Back to the real world. Have I shown you the poster for the gig?"

"No."

"Well, what do you think? We're calling the band Snots. Nice one, eh?"

Donal took the curled-up piece of paper Frankie had produced from his pocket and opened it up. In the centre of the poster a large off-green teardrop was printed. Over it in crude black and white was written:

SNOTS
WILL BE
APPEARING
UNDER
YOUR NOSE

and then, by hand, the name of the pub and the time. Donal laughed and handed it back to him.

"That must have gone down a bomb with Barbara's mother."

"Don't be fucking talking. She's even refusing to mind the kid so Barbara can't come. Anyway yourself and Elizabeth will be there, right?"

Donal nodded automatically, blacking the original plan to go to the pictures out of his mind until tomorrow, and went to the bar for two shorts.

"You're piddley-eyed," one girl was saying to another as they swayed on the high chairs.

Frankie insisted on getting another two and they knocked them back and stopped at the chip shop to get mints to disguise their breath. A stunted young kid with a disfigured leg was there, winning free game after free game off the Space Invader machine in the corner. They moved quickly past the shopping centre with its security guards and past the rusting gates of Gofton Hall, the old mansion across the narrow road from the main block of flood-lit shops with steel shutters pulled down like eyelids. The unlit windows and immaculately kept gardens of the house which seemed to exclude the noise of the busy street had fascinated them as children. The whole place had been cloaked in mystery with its occupant they never saw and its old gardener who ignored all questions shouted from the locked gate. Now it had been purchased by a property company who were letting it quickly disintegrate so they could knock it down. In the yellow light of the searchlights children were playing in a crater beside one of the half-finished functional blocks.

They hurried up the Meath Road checking their watches and, as they turned down the long laneway that tunnelled into the back of the factory grounds, they stumbled upon four boys who were taking turns racing a tinker's horse down the muddy path. While two rode on its back the other pair raced behind beating it with sticks to make the horse go faster. The terrified animal swerved to avoid them, throwing the two boys off, and they scattered them with flying kicks as the horse galloped away towards the camp it had been stolen from. The boys picked themselves out of the mud and chased after the horse, hurling back insults at Donal and Frankie from a safe distance.

They pushed through the evening shift milling around the clock, disturbing Jimmy in the midst of a probing run at two women who were slagging him, and clocked in just before the hand moved with a tiny jerk and the hooter blew. Dan was sitting alone in the cloakroom when they went in.

"Here we all are: the father, the son and," Frankie said pointing over at Dan, "the holy ghost. Or as they say at the folk mass, Big Daddy, Little Daddy and Spookie. How'ye, Grandad? Where's everybody?"

"The Lone Ranger has called a meeting up in the canteen to waste some more of our money. You smell like a mint factory so you'll be able to sleep it off while he's ranting away."

"Ah now, Grandad, times have changed since you were a nipper in the famine. That's what shop stewards are for you know. Don't be sitting down here like Cinderella."

"Shop stewards are to represent workers. That fellow is only a chancer. He was on the sites before this and then caused a strike in Cork. His only concern is to bring the whole place down in the name of the revolution. I've heard of that group he's in working their way up to the front in some peaceful march and leathering the hell of the police for ten seconds before vanishing. And the police and the marchers find themselves in the middle of a riot they know nothing about. Just see how long he will be here when this shindig is finished. I remember in my time . . . "

"Ah, in your time, Grandad, there was a statue of Cuchulainn up in the GPO and an old cobweb for a president. Have you not been there lately? We've a golf caddie for president and there's a statue of Pat Quinn, Supermarket King of Ireland, with a frozen chicken perched on his shoulder and a discount sticker for a shield."

"Get away out of that before I . . . "

45

In the canteen Donal woke from his thoughts. "Donal! For fuck sake put your hand up!" Frankie whispered beside him. He joined the growing chorus of hands that soon reached total solidarity.

"I knew I could count on you all," Toby said. "On Monday I will go back to MacCarthy and this time he will know he has a real fight on his hands."

With those words he moved down to the nearest group of men with that soldier's stride the men mimicked behind his back. The men moved past him with muttered words and nods and climbed down the stone steps past Duckarse who was checking the time on his watch at the bottom of the steps as they restarted the machines.

When he was going out Donal had kissed Elizabeth at the front door and waited at the gate to see her reflection vanish through the hammered glass as she returned to her mother in the living room. They would both be sitting there now watching the tail end of the late film. When Donal closed his eyes he could imagine the room with the light switched off, the warm smell of coffee in the air and the long coloured rays reaching out from the television in the corner like the strands of a spider's web. Beyond the curtains the caravan would be tucked up in darkness like a child's toy left out and forgotten about for the night. He prayed that she was thinking of him in turn as he pulled the handles of the slugger down for the first time.

Yeah, it was halloween in the factory
And we were all wearing masks.
From the fumes from the flux
And the dust and the gas . . .

An hour later Donal and Frankie were loading the hodder together, the loose handfuls of steel rods colliding into order against the metal back of the container. Frankie's voice rose above the machine:

The talc from the belt
Had discoloured my beard.
I was working the mixer
In the company of weirds . . .

46

The handfuls of rods were drawn downward with a clicking noise into a honeycomb of steel at the base of which they shot out in single file from the V-neck down through the pounding machine.

> The rods had been spilt
> And Duckarse saw red.
> The foreman had a halo
> Hung over his head . . .

Frankie spread his arms out in a posture of crucifixion.

> I was feeling real religious
> As I gazed at the hodder.
> I was strung up like Christ
> Between a pair of robbers . . .

"Ah, go on, Bruce Springsteen. I've heard the 'Night Shift Blues' before. Would you not think of doing a bit of bleeding work?" Donal grinned over at him and pretended to throw a handful of rods in his direction. "Here, your mixer is bubbling away. Slap it up there."

"As she said last night!" Frankie walked over to the egg-shaped bowl and began to wind the lid up from it, his voice following Donal as the younger man moved down beside the raised conveyor belt to take his place behind the shining metal tray.

> Well I know I'm a day late
> But there is no need to scold.
> I work a forty hour week,
> I just believe in parole . . .

Donal held his brush in the centre of the metal surface and let his gaze wander towards the other team loading trays of rods off their belt. A heavy thud boomed beside his ear and he jumped back in fright, then recognised Frankie's hand shovel which had preceded the flux over the high roller of the belt. He flung the shovel down the passageway after Frankie's retreating back, gathered the flux down into the hole in the tray and grasped the two handles.

47

"Who, me? No, it must have fallen from the ceiling. Besides, you didn't appreciate my 'Night Shift Blues'."

"Come on, Donal, where have my next round of slugs got to?" the operator called across the passageway. "You're not building sand castles now."

Donal ignored the eyes of the operator who was scanning the factory for Duckarse. The final slug rose, three-quarter sized and tough. Joe swung the slugs around and jammed them tightly down the machine with his steel pole, then slammed the door shut. The rods began to spill out again in a flashing stream like a shoal of flying fish.

Dan moved past the young man, pulling a trolley stacked high with rusted empty trays and parked it silently beside Jimmy and Milo. He worked at his own pace; the night shift had become harder in the last two years. If he stacked up enough trays to do them for half an hour – and they were unlikely to break their backs using this load – then he might be able to slip out into the cloakroom for fifteen minutes to rest. When he paced out his work like this he was able to reach half seven without experiencing any stomach cramps. He slid the trolley under the loaded pallet and pumped it up, then straining his long arms behind him, began to drag the delicately balanced load up the factory floor. He swung it smoothly into the gap in the storage section and parked it with the unconscious grace of experience. Duckarse had emerged from the door behind Donal and so Dan hesitated for a moment and then slipped out the door of the loading bay to make his way unnoticed around the outside of the factory to the cloakroom. From across the black unloading bay he could hear the cry of a horse and the sound of youngsters' voices. He pushed aside the heavy plastic strips covering the entrance and stepped out into the night.

With a sharp click the clock behind Donal reached two fifteen. He turned and watched the next load of flux come tumbling towards him over the top of the belt. He gripped his brush and remembered as he started to work. This time a year ago he would be leaving the Grove with Elizabeth; Rory Gallagher or Thin Lizzy or Status Quo, something heavy like that building up the crowd into a final frenzy of limbs before the whole floor was quickly swamped by a cold shower of light, dazzling the dancers, with everybody speaking too loud as they tried to adjust to the buzzing silence, and couples standing back to see each other clearly for the first time. Or maybe, if he was lucky, they would be emerging from the vast sea of coats with the very secrecy of the act having made it more exciting. They'd get a taxi down to her mother's, and the funny thing was that he would have walked down this quiet road past the factory on his way home in an hour or two's time. Often, if Elizabeth was sure her mother was asleep, he'd walk in the exhilirated afterglow of sex, his legs still trembling slightly and his mind contracting as if in sympathy with his body. The shadows thrown out by the factory lights were mysterious; his footsteps crunched on gravel and whispered over grass as he'd pass the heavy trees behind the railings burdened down by the splashes of white blossoms in the dark.

The smell of the trees on the corner always reminded him of childhood, the odour of baking bread filling up the street from the windows of the bakery. The night seemed to exist in a separate world, like a coin of daylight tossed on to its reverse side. The steel moon dying everything bluish-grey after rain, the trucks showering his body with cold air as they passed, the rivulets of oil spilling into rainbows of colour in the flooded gutters.

He had often stopped here, hidden by the shadow of the gates, and thought of a look on her face that he had never been able to grasp, perhaps because it contained too many levels to be explained. She would lie back, jeans at her ankles (she would never take them off fully), blouse unbuttoned to reveal the unbelievable pinkness of her nipples, and watch him unrolling the condom. Part of the look, he knew, was anxiety, part attentiveness for the upstairs creak of floorboards, part pure desire, but behind her softness a sense of somehow being above and in command of the whole affair, the unintentioned and unaware arrogance of a much older woman. And, sure enough, even though she might have stalled or made excuses before that moment it was always she who pulled him those final few inches down to her schoolgirlish body, giving way before him but suddenly moving with a soft wordless cry into a world into which he could not follow, absorbed in a total implosion of herself. She seemed to experience a pleasure that was more intense and pure than his, as he withdrew just before he came, already moving back from her when he was overcome

49

by a sensation of heat and pleasure followed by a helpless and tender weakness. Her look was gone then, replaced by a tired glow of wellbeing and a slow red blush spreading over her white cheeks.

In those days, standing among the pin-stripes of shadows from the railings, possibly dumping the used sheath in a tissue between the bars, he had imagined these factories to be like lost Egyptian tombs humming floodlit and vacant in the night. The memory came back to haunt him — "fool, fool" — as he gripped the handles with his aching palms, his eyes following the needle to seventy tons, the body releasing the handles automatically. He could see Frankie singing to himself as he mixed the next batch of flux, grinning and stoned. Three joints beforehand carried him through, he told Donal. Three joints steering him through the night towards dawn's desolate horizon. Donal's hand dropped the fragment of wire stealthily into the flux. It was the first time he had caused a breakdown without being told to. When the unexpected jamming screech of the machine scraped across their nerves the men on the conveyor belt looked up startled. Behind him Donal could hear the patter of the chargehand's feet. They looked at Frankie who shook his head and they turned towards Donal as if having to regard him independently for the first time.

* * * * * *

Dan had been standing for twenty minutes in the tangle of shadows beside the wire fence. Against his will the cry of the horse had drawn him through the parked lorries over towards the red spurts of flame glowing in the wasteground beside the factory grounds. The man's body was rigid, at first from shock and then from an automatic sense of survival. There were holes cut in several parts of the fence and if he moved quickly they could catch him before he reached the side door. Six boys were gathered around the fire on the wasteground, three of them warming their hands over it while another two were kicking a sweating horse which refused to move. The last boy was tugging at a rope which was tied around the horse's neck. Dan thought that it was only as a joke that the boy threw the rope over the branch directly

50

above the fire, but the other five had misunderstood and, after staring at each other for a few seconds, each afraid to lose face by showing either fear or compassion, they began to pull at the rope. The horse sprang to life and started heaving back and it was as much as the six could do to hold on, but gradually they began to wear down the horse's strength, which was already depleted after the long hours of riding. In slow motion, it seemed to Dan, its forelegs began to rise from the ground as if in a rodeo. It screamed an almost human cry, exposing gleaming white teeth saturated in a foam of sweat, and kept tossing its head frantically from side to side.

"Kick them, damn you. For Christ's sake charge at them," Dan cried silently as he pressed himself further back into the shadows.

Slowly the horse started to keel over to one side and then, in an instant, the four legs rose into the gleaming air, and it hung kicking out and tossing as it revolved on the rope with its hind legs suspended just above the flames of the small fire. The boys secured the rope to the base of the tree and stood back with a mock cheer as if uncertain what to do next.

Dan was torn between a desire to run for safety and a loyalty to the tied horse that bound him to the spot. Something in the big animal's helplessness reminded him of the moments of that English girl's lonely agony that he had run away from before. Dan was shivering and discovered there was a cold sweat on his face. For a moment he was almost overcome with a retching in his stomach. A sickness went through him in a shudder: at the minds of the well-dressed boys who refused to admit feelings, at the horse for refusing to attack them when it could have, at his own cowardice.

But what could he do? The boys would not be frightened of one old man. At best he could get off with a couple of broken ribs. If he reached the factory would the men stop the production lines to help? And how could he explain his presence outside the factory in the first place? Indecision now as always. The choices juggled and missed. Everything he had missed once that would never be repeated. Forever and ever, amen.

He ducked back into the shadows and ran around down the laneway to the phonebox on the road outside. The inside of it was like an empty shell washed up from a wreck. He moved back down the lane

51

with the factory rising like a black dilemma before him, then slipped in through the side door and down the waxed corridor, checking the locked doors of the office. He found a phone in reception and gave the details quickly to the policeman on duty, refused to give his name and put the phone down quietly. He knew he should go back to work now before he was missed. Even though he had worked with Dominick for years he knew that, having risen from the ranks of the men, he was now in mortal terror of doing anybody a favour.

Yet despite this, and the fact that there was nothing he could do, he found himself, almost as an act of penance, following the cries of the horse back to the fence, and standing there in the shadows, witnessing the complete act, never once taking his eyes off the horse's suffering as he recorded each detail purely for himself. The scene could be seen clearly from the roadway. Occasionally somebody passing would stop in shock for a moment and then hurry on. But most walked on the far side of the road with a staged and deliberate casualness, blatantly avoiding the scene with their eyes. Dan stayed there until the youths had gone home and the horse was dead. Near the end he hoped that the horse might be able to see him through the haze of blood, standing there cold and exhausted but somehow sharing in the pain, bearing witness in a silent and helpless testimony. But even though the horse's head hung facing him when it finally died, there was no spark of recognition or forgiveness that he might take with him as a consolation. No police car came. Dan remained in the shadows.

* * * * * *

The mid-Atlantic voice of the pirate disc jockey had little competition in the canteen. The four previous nights had taken their toll on the men. Many of them had succumbed to the habit and temptation of a Friday evening and the effects of the few pints were now being felt in headaches and exhaustion. The memory of yesterday's pay packet being only two-thirds of what it once was still rankled in their minds. Yet Donal noticed that it was at times when they were most down that the men seemed to team together with banter and slagging to pull each other through. Even those men who didn't especially like one another were bound together in a unity different from any Donal had known before. When you were tired they carried you. When they were down you covered up for them. Their comradeship was a form of protection and an intense circumstantial friendship which operated as an unspoken code throughout the factory. It was what made their hatred of the scab so passionate. Donal wondered how long it would take for him to hate the quiet man sitting alone in the corner with such a violent sense of betrayal. He leaned forward to listen to Jimmy's son talking to Frankie.

"The best time to take it," he was saying, "is early in the day. It's like a little door in your mind opens and you lose all sense of time until you can just float for hours. Then you begin to come out of it around ten or eleven o'clock, just in time for your cup of tea and beddie-byes with the wife. I can't even remember Christmas week . . . "

At the next table Jimmy was holding forth over the remains of a half-eaten sandwich. Donal moved back to listen to him with one ear.

"The first time I went up to see the son in the Ballymun flats it was amazing. I thought I'd take a short cut through those houses at the back of Ballymun Avenue – or as they call it now, if you don't mind, *Glasnevin Avenue*. And it was like there were two different worlds. Here were all these nice little rows of houses and children on bicycles riding around one little universe, and then, a couple of yards away there was the first of the Ballymun towers. And it had boarded up windows and dumped cars on the grass outside and all these women and children sitting out in the evening sun on the steps. And do you know what? There was no bleeding way into it. They had them totally cut off with no lane or entrance of any sort. So if you were a kid in school friendly with some boy from the flats you'd have to walk over a mile the long way to get the couple of hundred yards to his home. I was standing there looking at it and this old geezer cutting his hedge, real retired police officer type, says to me, 'Are you lost?' 'Listen mate,' I said to him, 'I used to shoot rabbits here before this was even Ballymun Avenue and I often think it wasn't only rabbits I should have been shooting.'"

The man stopped and listened to what his son was saying at the next table.

53

"If I catch you taking that stuff I'll kick your arse," he called across. "Why don't you get off your arse and get your family out of those poxy flats?"

"Ah piss of with yourself, you old tossbag. Somebody should put you back in your matchbox."

"I wash me hands of you. You grew up big and stupid. I often think the midwife must have slapped your brains against the bedroom wall."

"Shut up out of that or you'll have your balls for tonsils. One dig from me and you'd be lying green and red like a wounded snot in a gutter. I'm ashamed to have you for a father."

"Who ever said you did, you illegitimate little bastard?" Jimmy called over his shoulder, going out to the jakes.

"Ah go fuck . . . Dad! He didn't mean that, sure he didn't?" The young man's face had gone pale as he faced the grinning men.

Milo laughed at him and lifted his mug of tea. "He may be getting on, your old man, but kid, he's still miles ahead of you."

Donal left the canteen and climbed down the stairs to see Dan. For the first time he could remember the old man wasn't sitting in his usual place and his absence shocked Donal, as if it were some form of intimation. He walked through the empty factory, aware of Duckarse's suspicious stare from the foreman's high office window. It was almost four in the morning. The heart of the night. He stood beside his machine. A person trying to be nobody and to feel nothing for the next few hours. It seemed to him the only way he would learn to survive.

Suddenly he could no longer bear the chargehand's stare and he walked out the open door into the yard. He moved down towards the trees for a piss and saw the figure of Dan beside the wire. He started to walk towards the old man and then stopped, taking in the scene at the far side of the fence. The old man turned to face him and in the dying light of the bonfire Donal shuddered at the sight of his face. It was as if all the air had been sucked out of it and the skin was hanging in folds over the bones. Dan stared straight at him and neither of them spoke. Then he raised his hand as if beckoning the young man and Donal turned and ran in panic from the scene, back to the secure warmth of the factory and bent down to be sick over the choked sink.

When the machines started again he worked savagely at the slugger for the first hour, speaking to nobody and scrubbing away at the surface of the machine when the loads weren't running. Then all the fury seemed to drain from his body and there was just jadedness left. Even the animal power of dawn failed to rouse him from his fatigue. He worked methodically, no longer even watching the minutes click out behind him. At half seven they clocked out from the factory that was strangely quiet with no shift coming on to replace them. Donal saw Dan for the first time since break, standing in the crowd, looking pale and very old. Neither of them looked at each other as they moved out into the morning air.

On their way to the back gate Donal and Frankie stopped beside the crowd gathered beside the wire fencing.

"Jesus, Mary and Joseph!" Frankie said, "have you ever seen anything like that before, Donal?"

Donal said "no" quietly, looking after the figure of Dan moving away in the distance, and then walked on, and in that denial it seemed to him that a piece of himself died. He felt dirty and a coward and from somewhere in the Bible from school he remembered the words, "before the cock crows three times". Frankie had to run a few steps to keep up with him. Behind them the light wind was still blowing red sparks out from the black embers underneath the roasted horseflesh.

Donal seemed incapable of feeling anything as he turned the key in the front door and walked through the house down to the caravan. He stepped inside and stared dumbly at the empty bed. He reached his hand out in shock as his mind struggled to comprehend it and touched the sheets.

"Gottya!" He heard the giggle from behind his back as fingers pinched him. He spun round, weak with relief. Elizabeth was dancing up and down before him, naked except for a red-and-black striped tee-shirt, held down with one hand over her crotch. Her golden hair bounced back over her eyes as she laughed with delight at him.

"Want to swap jerseys, Captain?"

Four

I T WAS half twelve in the afternoon and still Dan could not sleep. Whenever he closed his eyes the bloodstained horse's head flopped and swung towards him, its lifeless staring eyes speckled with red clots. And always somewhere in the blackness behind it the figure of that boy, standing against the black outline of the factory and turning with a terrified look to run away from him. How the big horses had frightened him as a child, so godlike and powerful, stamping their hoofs and steaming after work. Now it hung, as obsolete as he would soon be, in the littered wasteground behind the rows of red-bricked houses, probably still not cut down. Long after it was removed it would hang like the dead weight of a crime between him and the boy, a wound that he would never dare to open and heal.

On Saturdays, since he had given up Legion work a decade ago, he used to visit some of the men with whom he had worked or shared digs in the fifties and sixties, but now they were all dead or retired. They lived out their final days on pensions in one-room flats like this one, walking with sticks to the local grill for the lunch-time special: watered soup, food with a faintly used taste and a bit of fussing-over from the young waitresses. A year ago in a cheap restaurant he had never gone back to he had seen a man he remembered as a leader of men on the building sites, bent over like a doctor doing an autopsy on the remains of his meal. Dan watched him pretend to drop a coin on the floor so that the young people at the next table had to help him look for it. An echo of his voice, strident and purposeful at meetings, came back feeble and cajoling, trying to softsoap a way into their conversation.

Their flats would begin to run down soon after they retired; now they finally had time to look after them, but their hearts seemed to go when the days fell down like a pack of playing cards around them. Mostly they sat with the radio or a newspaper and visited the pub twice a day with an increasingly violent shaking in the fingers and an almost childlike sense of expectancy. "I'm seventy today and still on my feet," they said to anybody who would listen and lingered over their bottles of Guinness, trying to transform a simple drink into an occasion. The light went from their eyes when they shuffled back out into the street to resume their one-sided conversations with the agony aunts and farming reports on Radio Éireann.

Within a month of their retirement Dan would stop visiting, as if afraid that senility and hopelessness were contagious diseases. The bent backs and the sticks glimpsed at a distance and avoided afterwards haunted like ghosts, not from the past but from his future.

One o'clock. Seven hours to go. He rose from the bed and combed his hair carefully in front of the mirror, fixed his tie under his white collar and gave his black shoes a quick polish. Then he joined the queue in the packed supermarket, a plastic basket holding his food for the weekend. Piped music smothered the cries of children. Large mirrors along the walls doubled up on him; behind them store detectives watched his movements.

After lunch he walked into town through bursts of mid-afternoon sunlight. With luck he might meet somebody in the Garden of Remembrance or on the rectangle of seats under the blackened angels of the O'Connell monument. The streets were packed with shoppers and youngsters hanging around. He passed through the blare of loudspeakers and sellers of republican newspapers in the portal of the GPO and, on the spur of the moment, walked into one of the amusement arcades beyond it. Down the back, under the intense artificial light, the rows of gleaming slot machines were arrayed, gods demanding to be served. The men and women stood without speaking, feeding coins into the slots under the eyes of the security guard. Occasionally the rhythm was broken by the bright clamouring of coins colliding as they tumbled down the winning slot. Nobody looked over at the winner, who immediately piled her loan into neat stacks to be fed back in. Dan hated this place and hated himself for doing so. It was the side of him that was terrified of risk, even if it were only a few coins. But once he had begun he knew he could never stop. He would stand here until every penny was gone and he could bask in the security of misery that only those with nothing can experience. The abdication of responsibility. An old man was eyeing him with an old familiar dislike. He walked out and the reflection vanished with him from the full-length mirrors.

He crossed O'Connell Bridge and stood near the old man selling papers outside the film centre. Across the street six wrecked phone boxes were lined up as if a firing squad had torn them to pieces. Boy prostitutes leaned over the Liffey walls in tight jeans outside the public toilets, their eyes watching the sluggish brown waters patiently. After a pause one followed a man inside. A Christian Brother came out, blinked several times in the sunlight and hurried away. Two cars nearly collided at the traffic lights and, as all eyes turned to look, Dan found himself slipping in through the door of the cinema, past the bored ticket-girl and into the hushed twilight of the deep seats.

As his eyes adjusted to the darkness he could make out the figures around him. The cinema was quarter-full, the men mostly middle-aged and alone, with a scattering of young converts who had bluffed their way past the usher with copies of *The Irish Times* parked under their arms to add the necessary years to their appearance. There was a silent intenseness in the picture house which reminded Dan of the men's mission at home when he was a child: the rows of men in the dim candle-lit church, the conspiratorial tones of the man-of-the-world priest leaning over the pulpit. There might have been a plot in the film once, but the censor had reduced it to nothing. The film jerked towards its conclusion in a series of dubbed slow build-ups to scenes in beach houses and the back seats of cars that were cut as soon as they began. The actresses displayed insatiable appetites for hygiene, with whatever plot there was being stopped every few minutes to allow one of them to strip for another shower. Dan suspected that the other men's emotions were led, like his, down endless cul-de-sacs, but he knew from the familiar faces that they would be back next Saturday, needing some foothold, no matter how slim, to haul them through the coming week. As the credits rolled and the chirpy foreign jingle filled the cinema most of the audience rose and left together. Those who wished to leave less conspicuously waited for a moment

59

and then as they rose to go were caught out by the opening strains of the national anthem. The older men stood there, confronting each other in the full glare of the house lights until the crackling music was over, trapped between their guilt and instinctive stirrings of old pride.

The young man sitting beside Dan on the bus home wore a pair of Auschwitz-chic pyjamas and a haircut that would cure headlice. The two youths in the top seats spoke Irish in raised self-conscious voices, halting occasionally to correct each other's grammar in quieter English. The girl sitting with them wore a long peasant dress with her hair tied in a long plait at the back. Her voice, filled with the alien tones of the rich suburbs of her upbringing, grated over the language of his childhood. He thought back to the women gathering seaweed in a frozen dawn and the young girls hiring themselves out to be pawed by rich farmers and sent picking potatoes in the frosted-over muck. Only somebody who had never seen these things would willingly wear the clothes of a peasant as a badge of reproach to the rest of the world. Was it the very fact of their youth or the haughty righteousness and fervour of their belief that bothered him, he wondered, as he cursed them under his breath in Irish words they would never have heard.

* * * * * *

Donal was up and dressed and had tea waiting for her when Elizabeth came home from shopping. He sat in his bare feet on the edge of the bed while she lazed in the armchair beside the rotating artificial flames of the heater. The sense of expectancy that had been a part of their Saturday nights since they were fourteen was building inside of them. He wanted to tell her about the horse, but there seemed no way he could do so without making himself appear a coward for running away from the old man. Already he was placing the incident in the back of his mind to be suppressed along with the rest of the nightmare of the night shift. Elizabeth jumped out of the chair and began to pace restlessly around the narrow space of the caravan. Donal held his hand out and smiled and she bounced down on to the bed to wrap herself around him.

"You're like a giant teddy bear, all warm and cuddly," she said, stroking his hair and kissing him on the forehead. Then she bounced her head back against the pillow, swung her legs up into the air and laughed.

"We should rename this place Wanderly Wagon: 'Here comes the Wagon, Wanderly, Wanderly Wagon, All kinds of everything, To make your dreams come true.' We even have a fairy godmother watching over us from the house."

Donal grabbed her and pulled her back on to the bed beside him.

"The way you're swinging around it's closer to a circus wagon."

She pushed her nose up into his face and said in her little-girl-lost voice, "Oh please, Mr Ringmaster, let me have a job in your circus. I'd do just anything except I can't be on the trapeze because I'm four months pregnant."

Then she raised herself again on her arms and suddenly her face nosedived down to bury itself in his jumper.

"Jesus, Donal, this caravan is like some sort of limbo. I wish somebody would just give me something to do before I crack up. You know, I never realised until lately how much of my own life I've given up. The whole world seems to have come to a full stop. I was silly to stop looking for a job when this happened, although it's a bit late now. You know, I'm so happy with you here, Donal; I've never been happier in my life. The most important thing in the world is for me to be your wife, but I don't want to be just your wife. It will be different when Mammy is able to mind the child and I can start looking again. It's just so frustrating waiting around here for it all to happen. Anyway it's Saturday night. Let's get the hell out of here and go somewhere special. Come on, Donal, suggest something exciting and we'll hope the fairy godmother hasn't the caravan bugged."

He was silent for a minute and she could see him biting his lower lip. Then he said, "Frankie is playing a gig with a band in town tonight and I sort of promised we'd go."

"What do you mean you *sort of* promised? Have you heard them play?"

"Nobody's heard them play. It's their first gig. They're a new wave band and Frankie is doing support and then joining them for the closing numbers."

"It's not in that awful kip in town, is it?"

"Ah, I promised Frankie we'd go, Elizabeth. He's been a good mate to me and he's a good musician as well. He played the Milky Way in Amsterdam. I feel I owe it to him."

"Jesus, Donal, do you owe anything to me? I sit here at home all week waiting for you and you owe it to Frankie! Have I an opinion? Do I get consulted about my evenings out?"

She jerked herself up from his arms and pushed the clock off the table with a loud crash on to the floor. Then she put her head in her arms and he could see through the folds of her hair that her face was bright red. He put his hand on her shoulder and she shook it off and rose from the bed, picking the clock up from the floor and holding it as she stared out the window. Then as quickly as the outburst had flared and terrified Donal she seemed to regain her composure. She grabbed a pillow from the chair and flung it at him.

Pouting as if to tease him, she said, "Sure maybe you should have married Frankie. Go on, of course we'll go. Sure Frankie is great gas. He's a superstar only nobody knows it. Do you remember the night he told us he was relieving himself through the railings of one of those houses in Leeson Street and he looked down and there was a queue for some pokey basement nightclub standing below looking up?"

And they began to laugh together at Frankie's exploits across Dublin over the years and as they talked Donal could feel the tension leaving her body. Then after a few minutes she leaned up on one elbow and said, "Frankie's important to you, isn't he?"

"He is, sort of. I used to hero worship him years ago as a kid and I still feel a bond with him because he's been through the same hassle as ourselves. And he did give me the tip-off about the factory job. Besides, I want to show you off to him."

As he rolled her over on to him and lay feeling the soft warmth of her body against his he felt a tremendous need to bind the two elements of his life together: to show Elizabeth that his mates were not just factory hands and dole merchants, and to show to the world that he was happily married by choice and not by force. He knew now that he would never tell her about Dan and the slaughtered animal.

After dinner they took turns to wash their hair in the bathroom of the house and dressed themselves in their weekend clothes. Having inspected each other they joined the hundreds queuing along the bus route. Their friends were gathered in small clusters on top of the bus and they shouted greetings and cheered when they climbed up the stairs. There was a festive atmosphere and an overwhelming smell of soap and perfume, the young schoolgirls trying to look older in pedal-pushers and split skirts, the thirty-year-old typists attempting to hold back the years by the simple approach of white skirts and flowering lace. Most of the passengers hummed along to the disco tunes coming from the young girl's tape recorder in the front seat. Donal put his arm around Elizabeth and she snuggled down beside him, her face radiant with a bright clear teenage smile.

* * * * * *

In the Saturday evening twilight when young couples were jostling in human snakes outside the cinemas and the older couples in the housing estates were warning babysitters before congesting the lounge bars and road-houses, all over the city pairs of hands that once joined in prayer were coming together to count beads of sweat in a slow rhythmic rosary of loneliness. After he woke, Dan locked the door and, having twice checked the curtains, unwrapped the brown parcel with the pound of lamb's liver. He laid it carefully on a dish beside the bed. Its smooth yielding surface would be gentle against his tired skin. He rose and took the envelope from the mantelpiece and Frankie's present from under the mattress. He opened the envelope first and was relieved to see it was the same girl who was in the catalogue. To postpone the moment he glanced through the stenciled lists that accompanied the photographs:

Dear Sir,
    Being a lady photographer who shares the same interest in candid adult photography as a few of my very private friends I am able to offer you, at our reasonable prices, these sets of highly detailed photographs taken exclusively for you in my friends' own

flats. These special sets of photos are here described by the girls themselves who will tell you in their own words the actual poses they have chosen . . .

Dan looked through the selections:

Girl Guide Uniforms, Stockings Only, Open Legs, Full Nude, Joan-Anne, Susan, Kay, Miriam and her friend shower together, Mother and youngest daughter, Really Fat Girl. I am sixteen years old and those photographs were taken now and two years ago. I have a lot to show you in these relaxed shots. Bye, Bye, for now, Helen.

He was disgusted by the whole circus of flesh offered before him. "I have a supply of used knickers . . . " What a place to find her in. But among the very lowest and most wretched she often appeared unnoticed and unaware. There were no more sets of Catherine on offer, if that was her real name. He placed the sheets of lists in the fireplace and carefully watched them until they were reduced to ashes. Then he lay down on the floor and pulled the old suitcase out from under the bed.

The statue he had carried with him since childhood stood sentry above the bed with a close guarded smile. The eyes were drawn down as if watching over him. He began to shift through the hundreds of photographs in the suitcase. Painstakingly collected over twenty years, the early ones were taken often from newspapers and travel brochures: girls lazing on a beach or posing at a deb's ball. But as the years moved on the poses grew stronger, the girls even younger, progressing through every stage of undress into nakedness. In very recent years they had grown more violent; the girls were twisted into positions of humiliation and pain. Yet each photograph contained the same long black hair, the same blue eyes with their mysterious hint of suffering understood, the same basic slender outline of features. As he laid them out on the floor around him they all looked like relations from a single vast family, or like hundreds of images of one woman, drawn from memory by different men. Dan had to kneel to spread them all out around him.

Hail Mary, full of grace, through all these years your eyes have watched over me. And I have seen them move from the cold marble robes of statues to gaze out from bent shapes in every form of torture in centrefolds. When I once touched stone, Mary, now I run my fingers over paper. And yet no matter how great the terror or the indignity they still will not come to life. I have never felt the sign of your tears dampening the paper or of your stigmata glistening on the stone. I am too old to change now. I want life. After all these decades of waiting and of staleness I need to have lived.

For decades I have waited for your revelation. When country girls were calling at parish dances on Saturday nights I stayed alone in that alcove held by the promise in your eyes. In Dublin and in London I waited patiently for that sign. I visited the sick and the old, worked for the Legion on summer evenings when each muscle of my body ached with desires I held in check. When my body thirsted for life I kept faith in you until my love was twisted into every crooked shape like a plant that has no room to grow tall in the sunlight. But the stem has never snapped. It still holds true. I have waited too long for a sign from heaven. Before I die, Mary, grant me a sign on earth.

Don't you know I am terrified that my death will be the same slow drop into emptiness as when the fever of hands dies and these walls form a tomb around me. When my breathing returns to normal all I have left to live for is the secret promise hidden behind your eyes to hold on to like a rope that might lead me to safety now and at the hour of my death, amen.

* * * * * *

The backroom of the pub looked as if the owner had begun to renovate it and then abandoned hope midway through the operation. Drink was served from a small hatch at the end of the room and a few torn chairs were arranged around formica tables in the centre of the floor. One yellow and one red spotlight glared down from the bare-bricked walls on to the raised platform where the drum kit and amps rested. It reminded Donal of six pallets stacked together in a corner of the factory.

All the way across town the pair of them had been play-acting; Elizabeth hung on to him as he swerved across into a doorway, pressing her against the glass while he loomed above her and she pulled faces at him. They chased each other across the uneven surface of the temporary car park, dodging between the cars, and he caught her against the side of a lorry and gave her a piggyback out on to the street again, refusing to let her down as she screamed and blushed with embarrassment. They straightened up as they reached the pub in case she wouldn't be served for being under-aged.

Frankie and two of the band were drinking at a table beside the door when they came in. He rose and insisted on buying them drinks.

"It's a bit early yet," he said. "It will begin to fill up in a while."

They sat on the long bench beside the wall and Frankie asked Elizabeth if she ever woke up to find Donal pulling handles in his sleep. She laughed and told him Donal was smuggling out slugs of flux to raise the height of the caravan off the ground. Donal got him a pint and he went back to join the band who were sniggering among themselves as they looked hazily at the crowd.

Donal and Elizabeth kissed as they waited for the gig to begin. "I've a tractor outside," he whispered in her ear in a mock country accent. "Can I see you home or are you with your sister? I'm not after a good time." She kicked his foot and told him she was warned about married men.

At a quarter past nine life began to stir among the band who were sitting drinking near the stage. There were now almost forty people gathered together in the extension. Most were friends of the band who mingled with the few brave explorers who reposed their hopes in attending first gigs out of curiosity or masochism.

After much encouragement from the band Frankie climbed on to the platform and began to tune up. Nobody paid him much attention. He stood looking in front of him until relative peace had settled down, started the introduction to one of his own songs and then seemed to change his mind.

"Well it ain't no use you sit and wonder why, babe . . ."

He sang Dylan in a low nasal tone with his head down away from the mike. Looking at him standing alone in the glare of the lights

Donal was amazed to remember how small he was. He seemed lost on the empty stage. His fingers were stilted unlike whenever Donal had heard him play in his house. Frankie finished the first number and walked quickly off the stage.

They could see him say something to the band's puzzled faces. Then the drummer jumped on stage and began to warm up with a loud clash. The lead and bass guitarists finished their cigarettes and joined him. The singer – or at least that seemed his function – climbed up and began to roam the stage at will, staring at people and pulling faces. He had a podgy, stoned expression as if he were indignant about something which he couldn't quite remember. His hair stood up in a stiff tuft at the top of his head. The crowd began to move back from the stage as they experienced a sensation of wetness after he walked past foaming into the microphone. Only when he stopped and turned to give them a cold intimidating gaze, pointing with his finger down towards the hatch where a barman was rinsing glasses with his eyes raised to heaven, did they realise that the band had begun playing. The neutral section of the crowd was aready starting to drift back to the jukebox in the lounge. Donal could feel Elizabeth's eyes watching him in bewilderment as they stood near the edge of the stage.

"Give them a few minutes," he said, "and then we'll split. I want to see if Frankie is going to come back on."

He felt embarrassed as if he himself in some way had been found out. He could feel her begin to move her body slightly, trying to find some rhythm in the music to dance to, and pretending for his sake that she was enjoying it.

The band had been playing for seven or eight minutes without appearing to find any natural co-ordination when the lead singer stalked off with a final large spit at the remains of the crowd. The bass guitarist called after him and he shook his head. The crowd cheered as he too put down his guitar and abandoned ship. Donal noticed that Frankie had disappeared. Looking up, the other guitarist noticed they were gone. He glanced around frantically for a familiar face before unplugging his amp. As Elizabeth and Donal walked towards the exit the drummer was setting an even faster pace, oblivious to the silence around him and totally wrapped up in the music inside his head. "Or else." as Donal said over his shoulder, "stoned."

Elizabeth giggled and said, "I think the Snots have all been wiped away."

They met Frankie on the way out, pacing the hallway with a cigarette in his hand.

"The crowd never gave us a chance," he said. "The lads were just beginning to get it together. Now the bollox of an owner is refusing to give us our deposit back."

"You mean you had to pay the pub to play here?"

"Well, that's the way it goes for a first gig," he said defensively. "Listen, you can't just go home like that now. Come on into the bar and have one for the road."

"I don't know. What do you fancy doing, Elizabeth?" Donal said looking down at her.

"I don't mind, Donal," she replied quietly. "It's your decision."

At heart he knew she did mind, but he couldn't bear the prospect of returning to the empty caravan on a Saturday night after all the hopes they had set out with. And so they went into the bar for one and then Donal had to get one back, and after that two of the band joined them and began to chat up the three girls beside them, and it was just like old times: knocking back pints and swapping jokes and luxuriating in the warm haze of drink and smoke and background music. Elizabeth seemed to be enjoying herself as well, joking with Frankie and slagging the boys in the band. And when he whispered to her that they would splash out for a taxi home from the pub, she looked at him with a familiar smile and nodded, saying, "Whatever you say, Donal. We'll go home whenever you want."

* * * * * *

Dan watched the crowds spilling from the pubs, complete with six-packs in brown paper bags, as he walked back towards Phibsboro after buying the early edition of the *Sunday Press*. He felt drained and wasted inside as he always did afterwards. It was just past midnight, a secret time for him when he first arrived in London after the war.

The city had been so vast, like a dozen Dublins laid side by side, with so many different girls in summer fashions that he had begun to explore it, piece by piece, at night. When he was sure nobody was looking he would stop at the window displays of those fashion stores that had escaped the Blitz and examine the plastic models stood up there. He grew to know the various makes of models by their faces and watched them progress through a succession of outfits from the light fabric of summer to the heavier materials of winter. In some way they had helped to ease him into the new world he was encountering every day. Having seen a woman's outfit made it easier for him to relax when dealing with her in shops or buses, as if a bond already existed between them. The models in Dublin had never been the same. Despite attempts at gaiety they had always seemed lonely figures to him, left standing there alone in windows each night, watching over the procession of young girls outside Clery's, stood up by strangers and learning the rules of the adult world. Dan had often stood across at the GPO watching the girls trying to blend into the bus queue and at the same time stick out in case their boys might come and miss them. This was where they first learned deception, learned to appear calm and relaxed while inside the agony and humiliation raged. And though they would go home and laugh or cry it off, swearing never to be caught again, time after time they would be stood up by life itself: in interviews for jobs, in packed dancehalls and in the sterilised cleanliness of hospital wards. The secret was to keep the heart open, to keep believing in the fabulous hand to be dealt even if, like him, they knew it would never arrive now.

Those plastic models had patience. They never complained even when they were left as the one before him now was in Dorset Street, the body lying naked in the back of the closed-down shop window and the disconnected head staring out at him, bold and accusing like that horse he was still trying to forget. He turned away from the window, troubled by her disembodied look that stirred an old feeling of guilt he had never been able to shake off since childhood. It was a feeling that had come, like plate glass, between him and those he most admired. It made him constantly want to do things for them as if he owed them some invisible debt for their company. Always in the past there had been those people whose lifestyles contained an aura which so enraptured him that he would have done anything to be admitted to the intimacy of their friendship. Those who kept him at a distance managed to retain that magic image of fulfilment. With those who gladly took him into their lives he always experienced a sense of disappointment after a time, as if they were to blame for the anticlimax of the expectations inside his head. Disappointment grew into resentment which sought for a word or a scene which he could use as a betrayal to cut himself off again from their exposed world.

He turned the front door key and tried to climb up to his flat before the ten-second timer on the light switch went out. Music was coming through the ceiling with the sound of glasses being filled. He heard the front door open again and the voice of one of the girls. Two sets of footsteps came up the creaking stairs and went past his door. The house was coming to life. He knew there would be no way he could sleep for another few hours. He left the paper on the bed and went down again into the night air.

Anybody coming from Phibsboro could make out the form of a man standing beside the closed restaurant on the corner of the shopping centre. It was not a threatening figure that stood there without moving, but one which seemed to fit naturally as if its true place were among the black shadows and closed stores and the ragged paper flapping against the small wire fence in the shut carpark.

* * * * * *

When Elizabeth was in the Ladies and the barman was shouting "Time now, folks!" Frankie had said to him that they had better get the take-aways now and Donal had nodded as if it had all been decided in advance. So with six Guinness for himself and a large Coke for Elizabeth they found themselves heading in taxis up to the damp flat the three Galway girls they had met in the pub shared. Out under the stars in the crowded street filled with laughter and singing Donal had felt the familiar throb of the wild need for excitement take hold of him. Elizabeth had slipped her hand into his jacket pocket and come along beside him.

Now they were sitting on a cheap sofa in the living room while Neil Diamond sang under the skating needle of the record player. Two of the country girls were fascinated by the way the drummer and lead singer were rolling joint after joint and passing them around. Donal inhaled and the white sensation of lifting took possession of him as if his limbs had slipped their moorings inside his skin and were floating apart and coming back together again. The room was lurching around him as he offered the hot roll-up to Elizabeth and she suddenly snapped, "I'm four months pregnant, Donal, for God's sake!"

He began to sober up and wondered how the night's outcome had slipped beyond his control. Through the thin plywood partition they could hear muffled giggles and the sound of Frankie's voice and then a girl's saying, "Ah, don't be getting serious on me now."

A moment later the door between the rooms flew open and the third girl's head appeared screaming, "Merciful Jesus, help us! He's after saying he's a psychopath escaped from Dundrum asylum tonight."

Then she was pulled back inside, and leaning forward they could see Frankie lying on the bed, holding her arm with his left hand and clawing at the air in front of her face with his right one. He was growling from the back of his throat and as she began shrieking he released her so that she fell into the living room. He climbed off the bed and into the wheelchair beside the wardrobe and said, "Are we off now, boys and girls? I've a wife expecting me. They stole this from some party at a nurses' home last week. Will you no give us a wee push?"

The drummer began to wheel him out the front door through an ocean of curses from the kitchen door where the three girls were huddled. The five of them turned down the Rathmines Road with Donal and Elizabeth at the rear. He felt her giggle beside him.

"Is he always like this?" she asked.

But as the effect of the drugs and drink took full control of Frankie, Donal could hardly recognise him. Although the night had become cold he was still only wearing the jeans and sweat shirt he normally wore in the factory. Increasingly he seemed oblivious to everything around him as if he were being driven by a force he could no longer master. They stopped beside the large church with the cheese-green dome and the three boys went into the bushes beside the wooden cross

71

to relieve themselves. They could hear the drummer say, "We weren't that bad, sure we weren't Frankie?"

And they heard him reply, "No. They would have listened to you in Amsterdam, unlike this kip."

"Hold on, lads, I feel a vocation coming on," the drummer said and began to tug at the cross.

With a slight gasp from the opening earth the three of them uprooted the cross and placed it on the drummer's shoulders, then moved unsteadily out to join Donal and Elizabeth again. From across the road came the vinegared smell of boiling fat and they started to walk towards the chip shop. The drummer nodded to Frankie and the singer wheeled him in. Through the misted glass Donal could see a space in the queue clear around the dribbling twisted figure in the chair as people turned their backs and resumed their conversations with faked indifference. Then the drummer surged through the door into the damp heat staggering under the weight of the cross. He stood swaying in the middle of the floor. Frankie leapt from the chair as the crowd began screaming and shouted, "Hallelujah! I've been cured!"

The drummer dropped the cross and the three of them took off down Rathmines Road with Frankie shouting "Come on!" over his shoulder. Donal drew Elizabeth back and they began to walk towards town looking for a taxi, and to Donal, looking after the retreating figures, it was like watching a ghost of himself from just a few months ago, and he couldn't remember why he had imagined he missed these nights, that selfdestructive madness of drifting like a ship with no anchor from one party to another across the city. Why was he running away from the very happiness and security that he had always dreamed of, from the only love that could make him feel complete?

He put his arm around Elizabeth, noticing that she had begun shivering from the cold, and stopped when they came to the dark overhanging of branches beside the stagnant green canal waters. He drew her into his chest and kissed her.

"Elizabeth, I'm sorry," he said. "I hope we are both able to always say those words. I've been an idiot thinking that I could still have the best of both worlds. All the craziness of the last few years has just been a substitute for the love you've given me. Let's go home now.

There is nowhere else in the world I want to go."

In the taxi home she curled up against him and neither of them felt the need to speak. They went down to the caravan and as he held her in his arms to kiss her she jumped back unexpectedly with a look of astonishment on her face. Her hand went down to her stomach and she gasped again. She was breathing fast and her face was flushed when she looked at him.

"Donal, it kicked! It kicked for the first time! It's alive!"

Her features were radiant and her fingers trembled as she drew both his hands down on to her stomach.

"Jesus, can you feel it, Donal? Can you not feel the little legs kicking?"

Donal could feel the warmth of her skin under the dress and the tiny tremors of her excited breathing. And finally, just when he was getting frightened, what felt like the shadow of a movement like a distant vibration reached his fingers. He looked up to say something but Elizabeth was turning her body away and speaking to the child inside her as she ran both hands down the front of her clothes. Her voice was low, like a mother soothing a baby to sleep, and she seemed to have forgotten Donal's presence in the caravan. He stood awkwardly outside the scene watching her until she looked up and her smile admitted him back into her company.

After she fell asleep he lay awake for hours watching her face in the moonlight and relaxing in the warmth and softness of their tangled limbs. Looking back over the evening he saw how maturely Elizabeth had handled it, how quietly and confidently she had allowed him the freedom to come to realise that he did not want it. Now that it was over he felt that it was she, in some way, who had been running the night. Her face in sleep was like a calm ocean under which mysterious creatures swam. Donal was filled with an irrational longing to discover what she was dreaming about as if afraid that he was losing her to an unknown force in sleep. Her head was tucked into his shoulder and his arm ached under the weight. Yet there was no way he could move without waking her. So he gazed up at the outline of stars through the skylight in the caravan roof and tried to sleep. But whenever he closed his eyes a jumble of memories crowded through his mind. They came to worry him without any link in time or theme, crowding one after the other like random footage from an incomplete film that he had never been able to edit down into any sense of order.

Part Two

Five

ELIZABETH'S HAIR was blown back, fair and golden, by the light wind that wisped through it, flashing pure gleams of colour from its flying strands. She fell beside him in her green school uniform, flooding the blanket he was lying on with her warm presence and, rolling over, dropped a bundle of newly mown grass over his face. It had a moist texture, filling his nostrils with its fresh scent as he shook it from his hair and leaned up to watch her vanish among the lilac trees at the bottom of her mother's garden. The trees were in full bloom and as the birds concealed in the branches sang it was as if the clear notes were coming from the open pink throats of the lilac blossoms. A dog was curled luxuriously at his feet in the spring sunshine and a radio played far off on the window-sill.

May was the month of Mary, Elizabeth had told him, her childhood month of devotion and flowers. When she brought out the orange juice she took a blue straw for Mary and gave him a red one for Jesus, as if allowing Donal to enter into the secret language of her childhood. As he was cutting down a huge bunch of lilac for the house she showed him the sheltered clearing between two trees where each May she build a small grotto among the overgrown bushes. She pointed to the space with a sense of wonder as if overcome with nostalgia for a time she had barely left.

Beside the blanket a history book lay unopened. Six weeks in the distance the Leaving Certificate was a red line drawn across their horizon. For years it had hovered there and they had sailed ever closer. Now it lay in wait for them, an ordeal to be overcome in their separate examination halls, and who knew what rewards lay on the far side. A whole new continent opening before them of travel and of independence with a slow slope of years down to a new horizon of the possibility of marriage and families. Already the dead weight of those stifled years in classrooms seemed like driftwood on his life that he would soon be cut free from.

He tried to study but always her image would come between his mind and the page in front of him. When he closed his eyes at night he could see her hair being tossed back and her ready laughter at jokes he spent all his free time rehearsing to tell her. He discovered that he was starting to live events twice, once in the actual participation and again in the sharing of the story with her. Elizabeth was haunting his every moment; she was ever present like a rich sap that was seeping through his blood stream, like the lilac blossoms that were suffocating him with colour. She was his life now, everything that he cared for. When she came weaving out of the trees he ran to catch her, to spray grass over her running figure, and when she fell to hold her and feel each warm excited breath come trembling from her lips.

* * * * * *

Frankie and Barbara had been missing for eight days when the long distance phone call came to the neighbour's house. The voice seemed another world away over the bad connection from the London coin box. Donal was still breathing heavily after racing down the street from his own house.

"Here, I didn't phone you for a dirty phone call," Frankie said when he heard his breathing. "Listen, I've got us this small flat in London, Donal. A one-room place. It's all right. I've been looking around for a job on the building sites and Barbara still has a few quid left from her savings. We can hold out for another fortnight at least."

Behind him Donal could hear Frankie's father being restrained at the door. He had never held so much responsibility in his hands before. He found himself repeating the advice the men had told him to give.

"Come here, Frankie, you're after putting the shits up them all. Things have cooled down a lot since you cleared out. The lynching

78

party has been disbanded. You've shag all chance of making a break for it over there; you may as well come home. How's Barbara keeping?"

"She's grand. Not a bother. No, she isn't actually. I think she misses her mother, which is more than I'd ever do if I got her in the sights of a rifle. I suppose we'll have to face up to it one day. Listen, you can tell them you talked me into it, and make sure they slaughter the fatted calf and not the future son-in-law. Sure, it will be good to see yourself and the lads again. Anyway mate, I'll see you in two days' time."

Donal replaced the receiver and discovered that now it was over he was beginning to shake. He felt a sense of unease as if the choice had been thrust upon him and he had in some way copped out of the decision. He turned and walked out to the huddle of adults in the garden, exchanging cigarettes in low voices under the evening sky. In his mind he had a picture of Barbara, pale faced and already starting to bulge slightly under her coat, anxiously waiting outside the red phone box in the crowded English street.

* * * * * *

Most nights now he found that he couldn't sleep much before dawn. It had begun with the long parties and reunions after the final exams when there was no need to rise early the next morning. Then, slowly, the horizons of sleep started to drift backwards through the long hours of darkness. When he had lain awake long enough to know sleep wouldn't come he would turn the light back on and read library books while beside the bed the clock ate its way through the night with the persistent churning-up of time wasted. Through the window he would watch all the lights down the street go out one by one like spent matches until finally his small bulb alone was burnt out by the dawn.

Or often late at night he would close the front door softly so as not to wake the house and take the longest possible route to a post box half a mile away where he would drop a blank envelope down the slot, to keep up the pretence that there was some purpose to his actions, and

79

then turn for home through a different puzzle of streets.

Tonight even though he had taken the most indirect route to the post box he still didn't feel like going back to face that empty bedroom again. He walked on, out towards where the countryside broke loose from the eye of the last street light fading down the small road. He moved impulsively past the dark shape of an abandoned barn caving in on itself and down under the wildly swinging branches, picking his way carefully through the darkness. How little he knew of this world only streets away from him. As his eyes adjusted he could make out the hedges and pylons strung out across the fields. A swift terror went through him in the face of the solid mass of darkness, but he walked straight ahead like a man who had stepped out of time. Hours and days had ceased to mean much to him. What difference was Wednesday from Sunday when the major occupation was a card session that stretched through each afternoon? How could day be for work and night for rest when there was no work? Those school friends with jobs he could not afford to keep pace with, those who were studying were wrapped up in diagrams and mid-term assessments. Never had he spent so much time alone before. The years before him seemed to revolve in a long cycle of wallpapering and re-wallpapering his bedroom until there was only a small space in the centre and you turned the light off with a pair of pliers.

There was a danger, he knew, in having so much time. It hung around him like a heavy overcoat as he tried to keep abreast in this slow inward-growing whirlpool of days. Unless he took more and more drastic steps to keep blocking it he knew that one day it would pull him under, with no sound coming from the lips that opened and closed just below the surface, and then his life would slot into one endless dull nightmare from which there would be no snapping awake.

He walked out through the darkness, past Dubber Cross and Pass If You Can, through St Margaret's, out towards Swords, and then he turned back past St Bridget's Well again. Each house was distinguished in the blackness by the angry warning bark of a dog as he passed which made him feel like some kind of criminal. He climbed the winding hill into the hamlet of Drumshoughlin and turned down the lane where the tall grained bulk of the castle pulled at the earth in the greying light. A white mist was drenching the fields in a cloud that seemed to hover above the ground, blending in with the trees and ditches. The light from it began to draw out the details of railings and telegraph poles. In the midst of his numb exhaustion he felt cleansed and complete with the light brightening over fields and scattering the darkness that lingered under walls and ditches, as if its pure unfocused whiteness were bathing away the hardened mucus of these wasted months. The moment was as close to belief as he had ever experienced, but in what he still couldn't establish.

Under the black calling of crows in the dense treetops at Kilshane Cross he turned down the main road towards the city. Every few moments lorries knocked breezes past him as they pounded the final few miles to the docks. When they faded again there was complete silence. The trees were starched and the sky laundered by the light. The only human thing ahead of him was a car half hidden under the overhang of wet bushes in a lay-by. He stepped through the plate glass of morning like a man released from the dark crypt of night and, blinking at the sharpness of dawn, he glanced through the back window of the car where a sleeping couple were parked in each other's arms.

* * * * * *

"I wanted to call him after the entire Arsenal first team, but the mother-in-law wasn't that impressed."

Frankie left him and went up to join Barbara in the front aisle of the church. There were eleven babies to be christened. What was that line he was studying for the Leaving Cert? "Fish, flesh and fowl commend all summer long." It made sense for a change. The eleven babies were the quietest people in the church. The adults clustered in little family groups in the first twenty rows, holding the younger offspring who dribbled and wiggled in their arms, while behind them the older children were playing cops and robbers and fighting over sweets. Donal could just about hear the voice of the priest over the squall of the assembled multitude:

"You will bring them home and feed them on rusks, but today we will feed them on something more important that will sustain them for a lifetime. We ask for them all, Mark, Joan, John, Mary, Francis . . ." Frankie grinned as he held the child with a candle in one hand . . . "Patrick, Lennon – Lennon? Well I don't think we have a Saint Lennon. Ah well, maybe this one will be, Helen, two Margarets and Susan . . ."

Relations swarmed all over the altar rails recording every moment with their cameras. A man in a heavy business suit panned his small cine-camera across the church towards Donal's row. Donal began his impression of a piano player on the back of the pew and the camera moved quickly on. Over the noise of his flock the priest droned on regardless like a young schoolteacher who had lost control of his class.

* * * * * *

The bus drove down a tunnel lane of old trees standing in a guard of honour outside the high walls of rich houses. At the corner it swung left and the sea was suddenly before them, with a rich vibrant blueness beyond the sawn-off cliffs that saturated his mind with colour. The shock was like putting on a pair of special glasses and surfacing into a world of soaked light, where he clung to the rail of the seat, overcome by the sheer closeness of everything.

As the bus began its descent to the bay Elizabeth turned excitedly beside him and hugged his shoulder with one hand as she pointed with the other towards the sandy beach, almost deserted in the bright summer morning. He could see the blood rushing through her white cheeks under that flood of golden hair that fascinated him. There was a warmth and togetherness about them in that moment which seemed to flash between their bodies like electricity, an emotion that seemed to him for the first time to be tangible.

When the bus stopped they cleared the low fence and began to race up through the tall unkept grass towards the hotel entrance, swinging out of each other and panting as they breasted the top of the steep climb. They straightened up before he led the way into the hotel lobby and Donal found he was almost frightened to speak to her as if, having exposed themselves like over-excited children, they were sure to quarrel over something silly and sulk all the way through lunch.

The dining room had once been a library. Leather bound books locked behind glass cases lined the walls. A chef dressed in a comical white hat poked his head out of a hatch and gave them a grin. The menu was laid out like the contents of a book with the starters as a foreword, the main dishes set out as chapters, and the desserts printed as an epilogue. Elizabeth indicated her choice in the corner of the page and laughed.

"Is the Enid Blyton corner only for children?" he asked the waitress.

"Yes, sir."

Donal looked over at Elizabeth who started to smile and had to look down at her plate.

"Well my daughter would like it so."

"We must pass the Leaving more often," he said to Elizabeth when he ordered a half bottle of wine and finally persuaded her to drink a glass of it mixed with water, in a toast.

"That's my confirmation pledge broken," she said, and when they rose to go she turned sideways and knocked a plate on to the floor. It shattered into tiny china stars, causing the other diners to look up.

"Never mind, it could happen to a bishop," Donal said leading her out the door. "Mind you, he'd be in a bad way serving mass."

Upstairs she got him a gin and tonic and an orange juice for herself from the barman who was eyeing them with distaste. They turned their backs and sat in the window seat enjoying the sea breeze drifting in past them. Below them the waves glistened back and forth along the brown sand and very faintly the noise of the tide reached them. If only they could be alone like this always no friction would ever intrude.

"That was really beautiful," she said. "Let's go down to the beach."

He took her hand and, at the door of the lounge, gave two fingers to the barman. They raced out and down the driveway, past the "No Using Your Horn After Dark" sign, and ducked under the railway bridge on to the pebbly sand at the start of the beach.

"Catch me if you can, my name is Dan, for I'm your man," she sang over her shoulders, running away from him. He chased her down the beach, sliding as his feet sank in the loose sand, and then they turned and Elizabeth chased him back up; but slowly the fun had begun to drain out of the afternoon as if the earlier closeness could not last unless it was consummated into some sort of bond. They played moodily along the edge of the sea, tugging and hanging out of each other.

"Go back waves, I command you! I am the King!" he cried, chasing a wave as it fell with a wet slithering noise down the drenched sand. As he turned to escape, Elizabeth was still running towards him and as they scrambled for a footing they fell wrapped around each other into the path of the wave racing back in over them. They lay there helpless in the cold foam, laughing as their clothes were drenched with sand and seaweed and the sharp tang of sea water, the freezing waves sweeping in to carry off differences, the shock of salt water closing and then teasing their eyes open.

They had to sneak back into the toilets in the hotel and try to dry out their wet clothes. It was late in the afternoon before they were able to get a bus back to town. The evening was so warm and close that they got off at the Grand Canal and began to walk aimlessly down along the bridges. The dark green water caught the heavy reflections of the leaning trees along the bank and the light on the path was green and shadowed. Ahead of them in the distance as they strolled arm in arm they could see the withered trunk of an old tree in a hollow with a steep bank up to the road behind it. Although the bark was gnarled and wrinkled like an old tombstone there was a ring of tiny delightful blue flowers growing in a semi-circle on the path at the base of the trunk.

"That's lovely looking!" Donal said, and they hurried up to examine them. When they came close to the tree stump they stopped and stepped back for a moment. Seen close up the tiny blue flowers were empty condom packets. Elizabeth bent to pick one up and burst into laughter. She showed it to him and he read the name of the flower, *Forget-Me-Not*, printed on the side of the packet. Elizabeth was still laughing, but for some reason it was he who felt embarrassed and uneasy standing there as if he, in some way, had been found out.

She noticed his discomfort and looked at him, then laughed again

84

and pulled him away with her small hands, saying in that young sweet voice, "Don't be so childish, Donal. If you've never seen one of them before now we're in big trouble."

They both laughed together and then Elizabeth asked him what bus they would take home, as if allowing him to resume command of their day. Over at the railings of the park the first girl was pacing in the summer twilight as they climbed up from the canal bank and watched the cars cruising along the ill-lit street.

* * * * * *

Elizabeth's uncle was the prior of the monastery and concelebrant at the wedding. There were twelve of her family and nine of his in the church. The only thing he could remember of the ceremony was thinking that the priest was an awful gobshite. Frankie was trying desperately to make a good impression as best man. He had even borrowed a suit from somewhere.

"Here, you take up that jazz and I'll carry up the other yoke," he had explained to the bridesmaid in a loud whisper when they brought the gifts of bread and wine up to the altar.

Both families were embarrassed by the whole affair. Afterwards in the dining room of the monastery they exchanged comments and compliments with an elaborate politeness.

"I would like to buy you a drink, Mr Kelly, but I'm afraid it is hardly possible in these surroundings," Donal's father said with forced joviality.

"No, no, indeed not," Elizabeth's brother laughed, "but the monks themselves make some lovely wines. Uncle Pat has been most understanding in the circumstances. But sure we're very fond of Donal . . ."

Donal stared out the narrow slanted window at the calm surface of the lake mirroring the wood behind it. The local priests had refused to touch the wedding. "Wait until the child is born," they said. "What difference can it make now?" A great deal to Elizabeth's two brothers, middle-grade civil servants with haircuts to open envelopes with. Employee, prospective father and bridegroom, all in ten weeks. The last three weeks merged into a haze of tight faces, family councils, whispers, strained gaiety and long silences. There was a sense of unreality about the occasion. He felt like a casual spectator at his own wedding, distanced from the voices rising in laughter and the clink of glasses behind him. A single bird was circling through the pale thin air of the mountains. A breeze suddenly set off a sparkling web of ripples over the lake. Even up here in the country it still felt like a Saturday.

"For fuck sake, Donal, get the lead out. What are you trying to do— catch the football results?" Frankie whispered behind him and put his hand on his shoulder to steer him around. Donal turned and went to join Elizabeth at the head of the table for the speeches. He took her hand and they smiled uncertainly.

The Sabbath shall be thy honeymoon.

* * * * * *

When he asked where did he start, the man took the cigarette out of his mouth and said, "You don't. There's a meeting up in the canteen. Come on up and join in."

In the battered-looking room there were about four dozen people. Donal felt overpowered at meeting all his new workmates at once. But there was still no sign of Frankie.

"Frankie, is it?" the man called Jimmy said. "Ah, now, it wouldn't feel like a Monday morning if that fellow was on time. Duckarse would think our young daddy was trying to spoil him."

He tried to follow what was being said at the meeting, but all he could grasp was that they would stay there until a promise was extracted from management about the position of the women workers. A long-standing arrangement had been broken, a confrontation forced upon them. A few of the lads grinned and nodded at him. The group in the corner scowled and looked through him. A middle-age woman smiled and winked across.

"Don't let that lazy shower put you on the slugger, son."

86

Later in the afternoon they resumed work and he helped the two men take the trays from the belt, placing them empty under the worn threads and then lifting them as the rods passed over. His fingers were turning to gold from the rust coming off the trays. He listened to Milo telling him not to wear his good clobber in this place and above the man's voice he could hear the sharp click as the clock's hand jerked forward every minute. Long rows of cards were arranged on racks above it.

"They asked you what in the interview?" Jimmy said to him. "You should have said you saw yourself in a bleeding mirror. What does it matter how you see yourself when you're only doing donkey work in here? Now, I tell you what I do every six months or so when I'm a bit cheesed off. I take a day off and go for an interview for a really menial job that I know I'm going to get. And I sit there and listen to all their shit and I answer all their questions, yes sir and no sir, and I wait until they have worked themselves up to doing me this great big favour with poxy conditions and lousy wages, and I suddenly stand up and say, 'Excuse me, gentlemen, but would you mind taking your job and sticking it up your fucking arse.' Then I just walk out and leave them to it . . ."

A thin rake of an old man, near his time, steered a trolley under the pallet of trays behind them with silent expertise and began to haul it slowly away.

"Get away out of that, Dan," Jimmy called after him, "you'll never smuggle it out the main gate."

* * * * * *

All that day it rained. He walked through the flooded streets, barely able to keep the umbrella straight under the force of water, to the station out beyond the last street light of the small town. He had taken an earlier train when he finished his first week's work at half three and booked them into the hotel overlooking the Mall. It had an aged, musty smell with rich well-trodden carpets and chipped antique chairs on the landings. A full-size mirror with gold-leafed edges had

87

surprised him leaving the room and he had jumped back as if caught doing something wrong. At the last moment he had chickened out and told the receptionist his wife would be along later, and had been relieved when she didn't smile.

He was an hour early in his anxiety, of course, as if by just being there he could somehow hurry the train. The single-storey station was in complete darkness. The whiff of urine directed him to the toilets. His shoes were drenched and after pacing the platform twice he walked back out past the freezing waiting room and through the late November rain into the nearest pub. Two double hot whiskeys later he moved back out into the cloudburst that lashed against the pavements. Although there was still no sign of officialdom the station was ringed with cars. Parents and boyfriends lined the platform awaiting the regular Friday night migration of civil servants and library assistants from the subcontinent of bed-sits and partitioned rooms in the hinterlands of Dublin. Elizabeth's mother thought she was at a volleyball tournament in Cork. Anything could have happened. Now it suddenly seemed crazy to hope that she would come.

Down the line lights began to change and the crowd pushed forward as the train pulled furiously into the station through the driven rivets of rain turning blue in the floodlights. She was there among them, caught up in a surge of suitcases and bodies, looking around frantically. He reached through the bodies and caught her by the shoulder and they kissed, a long kiss full of rain and waiting and the aftertaste of warm whiskey.

"I was worried. I wasn't sure you'd come," Donal said and she snuggled against him.

"Sure, we promised we'd blow your first week's wages. God, you're absolutely drenched. We'll go to Spain to celebrate if and when I ever get mine."

This weekend had begun months ago as a joke and a wild dream, and then simply as a chance to be alone and enjoy themselves. But in the last few days it had taken on a more serious note, as if it were a declaration to set out on a journey and travel so far to come back together again.

"Donal, I'm going to laugh. I'll never be able to go through with it," she whispered as they entered the hallway of the hotel.

"Come on. Just walk straight past her. She won't say a word to you."

In the room Elizabeth sat on the edge of the old fashioned double bed and giggled as its springs creaked under her.

"Oh God, sure the whole hotel will be able to hear us, Donal."

They moved out again through the blank wall of rain and managed to cross the waterlogged Mall to reach the cabaret spot. Two middle-aged men dressed as leprechauns were singing a song that began "Don't screw the coffin down till I kiss my dear mother's lips once more"; as the crowd grew progressively drunker they played livelier songs about emigrants and the dying words of hunger strikers. There was the loud clink of glasses and the ringing of cash registers and, every now and then, a voice in the crowd would take up the chorus of a song before the crowd broke into wild applause, fragments of their hands and faces being caught in the revolving coloured light with its hundreds of tiny mirrors. They took half an hour of it.

"Let's go back," Elizabeth whispered, her tongue like a small, warm animal nibbling at his ear.

They crossed the deserted street huddled together under a raincoat. From the hotel bar came the noise of glasses and singing. They slipped up the stairs unnoticed. Both discovered that they were shy undressing as if it were for the first time. And then Donal realised it was the first time he had ever seen her fully naked. The lack of limitations – her mother waking up and banging the ceiling or arriving home from bingo early, or somebody crossing the dark park – was a problem, as if they were swimmers who had swum out beyond their depth. It was the first time they were completely alone with nobody to answer to for their actions except themselves.

She looked across at him with her hair down over her eyes and both hands holding the rumpled slip to her breasts. He took the slip gently from her and, easing her backwards on to the bed, took her breast gently in his mouth. Somewhere far above him he heard her moan with a soft intake of breath. His nervousness made him need to assert his experience and extra year of age.

"It's not the same with this thing on, you know. It's not the same for me, that is."

He heard her whisper, very softly, as she lay under him, "You don't have to wear it for my sake."

The memories of all those nights when she had panicked half-way through and with one hand kept feeling to make sure it was still intact came back to him. It was as if Elizabeth were offering him her whole body and her whole person. *This is all I have to give you. Take it. It is yours.*

And despite the dangers that played in his head, despite the part of him that tried to hold back, for the first time their flesh met openly as equals. They moved on the tossed and shaking bed in a growing frenzy until they both came suddenly at almost the same moment. And although he attempted to pull his body away his legs were trembling into spasms and refused to obey him. He cried out like a man taking his final breath and collapsed, his mouth open, his eyes closed with unfocused colours merging before them. Her nose rested on his chin, her hair falling over his eyes. Sweat trickled down her face into his mouth.

They lay without speaking long into the night with the street lights sketching out the soft outline of the room, until the sounds of the after-hours drinkers had ceased, until the lights of the town finally died and in the total darkness only the rain poured against the window as if it had a stain that couldn't be washed away.

Six

June

A T THE end of Donal's first week in the factory when he had been put on the slugger, Dan approached him for the first time. The thin figure paused as he was hauling a trolley of trays down the path and regarded the new recruit. Then he looked up at Frankie and said, "Are you a friend of that scamp?"

"I am."

"Oh begod, we're in for more trouble so. You know, if he wasn't slagging me I'd swear there was something wrong with him. You wouldn't be up to him at all. Listen, I'll mind your machine and you slip over to the stores and get yourself a sweeping brush, just so you can be sweeping around the slugger when the chargehand or any of those flyboys from the office is passing. As long as they see you doing something you will not intrude on their consciences and you'll get along fine."

Whenever MacCarthy took it into his head to make his monthly inspection and the mixer was stopped Frankie would simply empty a few bins into a large heap at his feet and stand over it grinning with his sweeping brush until the danger was past. The first priority in the rule of safety was appearances. After recovering from the initial shock of his promotion to desk work in the office, Donal discovered that the basic rule was the same there, except that instead of a brush you held a phone in your hand and spoke politely into it until your superior had passed. In his case it seemed that almost the entire office staff were, or thought they were, his superiors, and in a few weeks he found himself more isolated than he had ever been in what MacCarthy called "the spurious camaraderie of the factory floor". When anybody

91

suspicious seemed about to approach he would discreetly dial 061 and replace the receiver so that the phone would ring by itself. He would lift up and tightly hold the receiver to his ear to drown the tone as he tried to weigh up the figure looming close to his desk. It was easy to bluff as the speech was the same to all the customers he had to deal with as junior sales clerk.

"Yes, sir, I'm afraid that the work-to-rule is still continuing in our factory. No, we've no news of a settlement. Yes, it is awful; however, we are doing our best to fill your order in the meantime."

Donal was shocked to discover that the office staff had no real understanding of what the dispute was about. When he heard it being discussed over lunch on the first day it had sounded alien to the one he had been involved in, but when he tried to explain aspects of it they looked at him with a kind of patronising suspicion as if he had been indoctrinated by a species from a different world. To the girls the factory was a place where they were wolf-whistled at on their way past. The men's main link was a football match twice a year. Management did not encourage contact.

It was Dan who had pointed out the notice to him as he did every time a newly typed sheet appeared on the notice board beside the sink under the foreman's window.

"Give us those handles and take a look at the board, Donal. The Sheriff has been in."

The Sheriff was a pimple-infested youth, fresh from school, who each morning exchanged a heavy mod overcoat and a scooter with a glittering flotilla of mirrors for an office-boy's white coat that was slightly too large for him. One of his primary duties was to patrol the factory, sticking up job vacancies for the industrial estate as a whole, under the constant hail of mock gunfire and the humming of spaghetti western tunes.

"Sure, I'm only in the job a few months, Dan. It's a bit early for me to be looking for promotion yet."

"Go ahead, boy, go ahead will you. Haven't you more brains than you'll ever use here and a good Leaving Cert. They're trying to cut back their staff for all they're worth. If they take you they wouldn't have to replace you. Don't say you wouldn't give your right arm to be out of this place."

And, of course, the old man was right. After a couple of months in the factory Donal's hopes of ever breaking free had begun to fade. When he had started first he had applied for everything, spending an hour each evening replying to box numbers in the evening papers. Frankie used to claim that if the Pope died he'd be racing over to personnel to see if they had the application forms. But now when he came home he was too exhausted to do anything except sit and look at Elizabeth's changing body as she sat there with two pillows behind her back to ease the weight, and worry dully about the future. Instead of claiming he'd be gone in six weeks or six months, he had begun to make excuses for the factory and invent points in its favour. But at heart he knew that the coloured talc rising from the belt and the dust blown in the door from the chemical bay were slowly choking him, the red and golden specks he was breathing in were settling in a cloud covering over his brain. All that night the old man's words were like salt irritating the wounds his mind had tried to ignore. The next day he filled in the long white forms and was called.

To the great amusement of the men Duckarse himself had to work the slugger for the forty minutes he was away. Donal changed into a shirt and tie in the jakes, replied with two fingers to the wolf-whistles from the lads and walked across the green lawns bathed in early summer light until he came to the single-store personnel building. He had been expecting one man to interview him, as when he joined the factory, but in addition to the personnel manager sitting behind the desk there was MacCarthy standing beside the coffee machine and a third, oldish man sitting with an open-necked shirt and loose tie on a chair directly behind him.

The three men talked and joked among themselves before they began to ask him about the factory. Donal noticed how they never mentioned the grinding dispute of the last few months as if expecting him to rush into the vacuum left in the conversation. He tricked his way out of it by talking about the composition of chemicals in the different fluxes, all of which he had spent hours learning off, but to his surprise he found that the technical facts seemed to mean nothing to the men. They quickly steered the conversation away again.

"Now, you obviously know your job inside out, Donal, but right now we are more interested in you as a person."

Under the combined attention of the three men Donal found that his nerve and self-assurance were starting to waver. When one of them asked him a question he wasn't sure if he should answer at once or wait until the other two had finished discussing some private affair. Occasionally two of them would begin to ask him a question at the same time or MacCarthy would walk directly across his line of vision when he was answering. In the end he began to lose his head slightly, and fixing his attention on whichever interviewer spoke first would answer him back aggressively, ignoring everything else in the room. He felt a resentment and a deeper sensation of being used than on the toughest nights in the factory. The interview had slipped away from him, he was certain, and he even allowed himself a joke when MacCarthy asked him if he was flexible.

"Oh, so so," he replied, flexing his right hand back and forth. He shook hands and stepped back into the summer light with a feeling of relief and returned by the longest route to the factory. The lads gave a ragged cheer when he relieved Duckarse of the slugger like a captain resuming command of his ship.

"Welcome back to the real world," Frankie shouted down from the mixer; "those fuckers have to sit down to piss."

Elizabeth was six months pregnant. Donal found that her body was changing in more than just weight: the breasts were becoming rounder, less like a little girl's; her face looked more adult, less ready to fly into laughter over nothing. They found themselves talking longer and longer into each night he wasn't working, as if they were only now starting to discover each others personalities and learn the true account of their pasts and their blind spots. Their relationship was changing, becoming richer like Elizabeth's body, but losing something of the swift infatuation of a few months before. And though they were more at home in each other's constant presence Donal could often sense a deepening tension within Elizabeth and, at times, almost a look of disappointment as if some expectation had been left unfulfilled by him, as if in some way he were failing her. He didn't seem able as yet to break down this barrier that he had imagined time would dissolve. The same fears were gnawing inside her, he knew, as the adventure of birth grew closer and began to black out everything else in their future with its eclipsing shadow. And at times now he felt himself excluded as Elizabeth lay with both hands on her stomach and her eyes closed as if communicating inaudibly with the child. At two and three in the morning they held each other in the narrow bed and invented lists of names, which they repeated into the night air and then rejected, unable to adjust to the sounds of them. Some nights she would wince as she developed a cramp in her right thigh and he would caress the hot skin tenderly until the muscles released her. But when he finally fell into a light sleep, exhausted by the day's work, she would lie there with her eyes staring up at the vague hint of stars through the outline of the skylight. When he woke an hour or two later he would find that she had the radio on, the rough American voice of the d.j. cutting across the night silence.

"Elizabeth, what's wrong?" he would ask, and she would turn herself full into the crook of his arms and Donal knew by the soft tremors of her body that she was crying. "Elizabeth, what's wrong?" But she would just hug him tightly and cry and never answer while he kissed her hair and held her close to him and knew that he would have to rise at half six for the early morning shift. And he was afraid to ask her anything else because he was terrified that she would not know his name or where they were and that in her helpless silence he would have to acknowledge the collapse of all their dreams. So they would both lie there, exhausted and longing for reassurance, with neither of them knowing the words that might penetrate deeply enough into the confusion of dark fears and beached hopes that bound them together and yet grew like a cancer between them.

One night she screamed in her sleep and he woke terrified and confused to find her holding him and sobbing. He put his hand out and switched on the torch they kept beside the bed. Her wet face looked up at him in the glare of the light and she smiled and cuddled up to him.

"It's all right," she said, "you big warm teddy bear. It was just a nightmare."

And then as if freed by the sudden shock of waking she began to whisper as she lay there against him in her pink nightdress.

"I dreamt there was a big spider in the house," she said. "All the family was gathered there for some celebration and, of course, I had to go around filling their glasses, and as I stood up from filling one I

95

could see it there squatting near my feet, with a sharp hissing and the front of its body raised up poised in the air. And I jumped back and screamed, but suddenly everybody was very cruel. 'Come on, Elizabeth, it's harmless,' I could hear Mike say, and then his wife said in a real scolding impatient voice, 'Pick it up and throw it out. Don't be such a child.' And I got frightened and ran upstairs to my old bedroom and locked the door, but they had built an air vent in the wall beside it. And I could hear their voices laughing as they came up the stairs and then Mike's wife said, 'Put it in the air vent!' And above the sound of their voices I could hear the loud approaching hiss of that big spider and I just screamed and woke up and . . . would you listen to that, you great clod!"

And Elizabeth stopped talking and Donal could hear across the darkness of the caravan the hissing of a tap which had been dripping in the sink all night. They smiled and when they kissed Donal could feel that her lips were hot and sickly and her skin feverish.

Often on those nights they could see the light on in Elizabeth's mother's room where she sat up knitting the bundles of tiny jumpers and socks that were starting to pile up in one corner of the box room. A cradle had been borrowed from one of Elizabeth's brothers, and a pram waited to brave the streets, on loan from a cousin of Donal's. Twice a week he crossed the suburb to visit his mother and father and try to figure out which of his brothers and sisters were talking to each other. While Elizabeth and he lay in the small caravan the world outside was giving its seal of approval to them. Elizabeth's family had adjusted to having him as a member and his older brothers no longer looked as if they could murder him. Once the formalities were taken care of a lot of tension had left the house. Any misgivings people had were kept to themselves. One evening when they came up for supper little Johnny had given him a sly wink across the table. Donal kicked him softly like a brother would.

"Donal, the Sheriff has been in looking for you," Dan told him a few days after the interview. "Run across there after him and I'll mind your machine."

The second interview was completely different from the first. There was only a junior clerk from personnel there. Donal was put sitting in a small office with a number of tests in front of him, most of which he knew from school — mechanical aptitude, spelling, sequences, grammar. He got through them all easily enough. When he finished he was handed a large folder.

"This one is called Choices," the clerk told him. "But you don't have to answer any questions you don't want to."

There were hundreds of questions, stretching for page after page. Totally stupid questions, each with a number beside it. Donal began to tick through the early ones.

I prefer:
A) Keeping my desk in work tidy   B) Watching television
A) Walking in the country   B) Washing the car
A) Going to dances   B) Playing sports

On the third page they began to change direction slightly:
I wet the bed as a child   (Yes) (No)
I like going to dances   (Yes) (No)
I look at dirty magazines   (Yes) (No)
I like washing the car   (Yes) (No)

As he worked his way through the sheets Donal became more and more angry. His mind was confused by the similarities and meaninglessness of the questions. He was reluctant to repeat the same answers over and over to almost identical questions in case he would look too straight a character so he began to vary his answers. One time he would like dancing, the next doing his job; the next time he would like kissing young girls, the next walking in the country. He was disgusted by the whole prying business which made him feel exposed and in some way dirty. When he completed the test he handed the folder back and began to walk out.

"Hold on," the clerk called after him. "There is still one test left."

Donal sat down and tried out outstare the young man in the suit. The clerk handed him a stapled form with two pages of instructions and six questions.

"You've two minutes from now," he said and then left the room.

Donal stared at the top of the first page. "READ ALL THESE INSTRUCTIONS CAREFULLY BEFORE YOU START" was printed in bold letters across it. It would take him over a minute to read the instructions before he even started the questions. Despite Elizabeth and the need for a job he simply could not be bothered with the whole affair after the last test. At least the lads on the conveyor belt didn't give a bollox if you were frightened of the dark as a child. He sat there in silence until the man came back and looked down at the untouched form.

"You're no fool," he said. "By this stage most people are struggling through question 3. Very few of them ever read the instructions through like yourself."

Donal flicked over the sheet and looked at the end of page two. "Ignore the following six questions" was printed there in small type.

"Ah, sure, I didn't come down the Tolka in a bubble." Donal grinned up at him and walked gladly out into the rich afternoon sunlight, pacing himself again to allow Duckarse's softened muscles to suffer a few final swings of the slugger's handles.

Although he had strutted around the factory for hours when he got the news, being ribbed by the men and having everything from lunch boxes to footballs sent up the conveyor belt to shower down on him, he knew, looking back, that it was the final test, if anything, that had got him the job. To be able to follow instructions carefully was a sacred blessing in these men's eyes. The Choices paper, was, he discovered, a lie test, a probing examination of whether you could answer questions honestly. As such he must have failed it and still got the job, which made him suspect that the entire interview had been cosmetic. The real reason he had been given it was for the wages they would save by not hiring an outsider. A young chap from the packing line of another shift had been transferred to replace him as slugger. He, in turn, had not been replaced.

As most of the orders were long standing and just needed to be confirmed and the company was unable to look for new markets until the dispute was settled he had little active work to do as a junior sales clerk. He had his own desk in the centre of an open plan office and, never having been used to one at home, jumped every time the phone rang. Most of his first two weeks were spent easing his way into the cloak-and-dagger world of company politics. People checked who he was and who he might be related to before venturing over to say hello.

If in doubt they walked past, appearing intent on their work and oblivious to his presence.

In the factory there had been no hierarchy beyond the simple division of those with white or brown coats and those without. Here there was a constant power struggle of whispers and perks that involved little obvious monetary reward but seemed to confer additional status and workload upon the victor. Those at the top of the pyramid generally left those beneath them alone or took a patronising pleasure in saying hello, but those stuck in the middle, gasping for the light of promotion, seemed to need to assure themselves of their superiority by asserting their superior positions constantly.

Donal's immediate superior was a man with a deeply lined and worn red face, as if worms had left their trails across its folds, who radiated a sense of having been bypassed by life and soured by it; it seemed that any inefficiency discovered in Donal's work reflected discredit on him personally. Donal could sense resentment in the older man towards his youth and his energy. The other great change for Donal was (although he had been one of the mildest spoken factory hands) modifying his language to blend in with the plate glass and clicking typewriter keys of the office world. His wages were not much better, however, as he still functioned under the firm's pay structure which, although demanding the same level of productivity, paid only a percentage of full wages, increasing by age until one reached twenty-one. Instead of wages he now received a salary – a matter of much rejoicing to Elizabeth's pen-pushing brothers.

In the two weeks he had been in the office the lads had been on evenings and nights and this was the first week he would have a chance to skip down to see them. He had seen Frankie once very briefly in the local pub, but he had been with members of Snots, who were still planning their second gig. Donal had tried to start a conversation but Frankie had been bombed and kept breaking into giggles and saying, "Look at his tie and shirt!" Their friendship had never recovered from the night of the gig as if Frankie resented Donal's presence, which stood between him and the version he told the factory. Although they were still friendly Frankie's grasp on reality had seemed to wander more in recent weeks. Occasionally he would arrive in work clean-shaven and talking sense in his piss-taking way, but then he would vanish for a day and arrive back singing to himself, making simple mistakes in his work and telling anyone who would listen that he would pack the whole lot in in a month's time. He was like an enlarged version of all those elements which people seemed to expect from him, out of which only rarely did the real person emerge now.

"You would have sworn Dan himself had got the job, he was so excited," Donal told Elizabeth on the evening he left. The old man had pumped his arm for several minutes saying, "Didn't I tell you so, boy," and then embarrassed Donal by giving him his address on the back of a torn Players packet and telling him he was welcome to call anytime.

"Now, I'm not asking you to call, boy. Don't get me wrong. I just mean if you are hanging around the area. I wouldn't give my address to anyone else in this place. We could have a good chat and a bit of a laugh. You might want somewhere to go after the little one is born."

The rest of the men had joined in the celebrations as well. Frankie had stolen a bottle of whiskey and kept it hidden in the mixer when it wasn't in use. It was passed around and added to the tea in the canteen. During break Donal had gone down to say goodbye to Dan and the old man wasn't there, as if embarrassed in turn by the earlier scene. The only ugly moment came when the forklift driver parked his truck near the slugger and began to climb down.

"Ignore that scabby bastard or there will be trouble," Frankie said in a harsh voice unlike his own and Donal ducked out to the jakes. Lately the blackleg's lunch had disappeared twice from the high platform where he based himself and his bicycle had been punctured. He took it all silently, counted his pay packet which was one and a half times that of the rest of them and wheeled his bike home to his wife and deaf-and-dumb child, a solitary figure walking in a large space that cleared around him in the throng moving out of the gates.

On that Friday Elizabeth and he celebrated by paying one of their pilgrimages to *The Rocky Horror Picture Show*, which had been running as a late night show every weekend for four years in the same cinema. By now the young audience who made their way faithfully to the out-of-town picture house knew every line and song in the film by heart. As soon as the house lights went down the chant "Queue the

100

lips!" began, and the red lips appeared and the cheering and the dancing and the mock riot began. The manager raced up to extinguish the rows of matches held alight at the back of the cinema while the front rows he had just left lit up again. When the action stopped for the obligatory professor in his book-lined study to fill in the details of the film the chant began to be taken up throughout the stalls: "Show us your dick! What's your favourite colour? Show us your dickie! What's your favourite television programme?" Donal had come prepared and as soon as the all-American hero (whose every word was greeted with "Asshole!") stepped from his car into the pouring rain, he held the newspaper over their heads as the whole cinema sprayed itself with water.

They took a taxi home and both fell asleep at once, exhausted by the excitement of the day. During the night Donal had such a vivid dream that when he woke he just lay for hours staring into space. In the dream Dan had arrived at the caravan door when they were getting ready for bed. Although surprised and embarrassed to see the old man he had let him in and introduced him to Elizabeth. He sat on the single armchair in a sullen silence, ignoring all their attempts at polite conversation until finally he reached up and removed his cap. There was a rash of swollen red sores covering his bald forehead where the hair had retreated. Donal had stared at them in fascinated horror.

"Good Jesus, Dan, what is that?"

The old man looked up and gazed right into Donal's face before he answered in a low and disappointed voice, "That is loneliness. What else do you expect when you leave me alone?"

101

Seven

WHEN DAN got home at four o'clock on Thursday from the early shift there was a social worker on the radio chat show talking about loneliness. He listened for a few moments and then, even though he hated the silence, ran quickly through the maze of jumbled illegal stations and switched the radio off in disgust. People like that spoke as if loneliness were a purely mental state. It was a pain as piercing and physical as the arthritis in his arm or the harsh tearing in his stomach when he exhausted himself in work; and like those it was a pain that Dan had learned to live with and to respect. He had come to know in advance when it was going to strike and could sidetrack it before it grew out of control. The worst moments were when an unexpected space came in his life, if he woke suddenly at night after a dream or he set out to visit a place that was closed and the whole evening was left, drawn out and empty, on his hands. Then as he walked back home through the streets the old ache would rush in to fill the vacuum and take possession of his body until he could feel nothing except the isolation and the barrenness of his life throbbing against his skull.

He moved over to the window and, keeping well back, looked down through the lace curtain at the petite figure with brown oriental skin who was studying below him. Nobody else had ever braved the weeds and debris from all the passing lives that littered the back garden of the house, but on the day after her arrival the coloured girl had cleared a patch for herself and now read her textbooks there in the evening, stretched out in a battered deckchair with her legs reaching from under a short black skirt to rest on one of the bin tops.

Dan always disliked new arrivals at first, as if they were invaders of the small privacy he had built around himself, but normally he found himself drawn into their lives. He would always be there with the loan of the bus fare or milk or sugar, taking it almost as a favour if they asked him. And although he knew most of the young people probably laughed when he turned his back, at least to his face they said thanks and made a joke or, if one of the girls were going somewhere special, did a twirl for him and kissed him on the cheek like an uncle. These were the small stones from which one could build a life.

He had lost both the young lads in the factory. Although he had convinced himself that he was delighted when Donal got the job the selfish part of him had hated the separation. He knew how quickly he would be forgotten, even if he had meant anything, in the youngster's new life. Frankie still came in most days, but he was as distant as Donal. His eyes had lost what light they once seemed to have and his humour, which was once so sharp and light that it hung like a kite the young man played between his fingers, was now the heavy malicious laughter of the factory. When he called Dan "Grandad" now it was with a bitterness that made the old man shudder.

Three weeks ago Dan had arrived home and met a young girl leaving the house with her dark skin highlighted by the white jeans she wore. He watched the jeans with the three blue fingermarks on the rump move down the path and then turned and climbed the stairs without speaking to the landlord who, wearing a pair of overalls to cover his uniform, was painting the hall blue. The next evening she had knocked on his door, explaining in perfectly phrased but slow apologetic English that she had moved into the bed-sit next to his and asking directions to the local launderette.

Since then they had smiled and nodded to each other when they met on the stairs or near the bathroom they both shared. She was a quiet neighbour who caused him no trouble and whose subdued presence, although young, seemed to blend with the slow air of decay that hung about the neglected house. She was starting university in October she had told him on the only occasion they had exchanged words since. Her sole visitor was a stocky muscular man in his late twenties who occasionally wore the uniform of a prison warder and spoke with a Mayo accent from under the rim of his bushy moustache. He called for her three or four nights a week and often Dan could hear them returning, her foreign accent low, asking him to keep quiet as they climbed the stairs; his loud with drink, filling up the whole house as if he needed to assert his conquest publicly.

Next door to them Dan lived on the edge of their relationship as he had lived on the fringes of so many lives. Lying awake with the moon pencilling in the room like lead around him he could occasionally make out sentences if they began to fall out. Her voice, low and tired, saying, "It's late now," and later, "No, not that way, that way hurts," followed by his strong laugh. Then a long silence would invade the house and afterwards, if Dan were still awake, he would hear the front door close and the steps echoing up from the concrete below to the pair of silent bedrooms, before the car started up for the short trip to Mountjoy Jail, or Kavanagh's Hotel as it was called when he first came to live in Dublin.

Even though it had happened to him a dozen times in the past Dan still couldn't pinpoint the moment when it actually occurred, but suddenly he had found himself acutely aware of the girl and every tiny thing she did, until his life recently began to revolve around her. There was that mixture of heart-breaking ecstacy mingled with pain every time he saw her which he had never imagined to experience again except as a stale memory; but here it was, clear and shocking, like the cool water of a well that had been overgrown for years. Now it was impossible for him not to be concerned for her and he couldn't understand what attracted her to the prison officer. She was an attractive and intelligent girl yet she seemed incapable of venturing out of the house by herself. Last week he had been woken by a short cry and then a door slamming. The next morning on the stairs she had regarded him with her slow smile as if pleading with him not to mention the small bruise discolouring her cheekbone. Late that night he heard her, very faintly, crying to herself. He paced up and down in the tiny room next to hers, as apart as if they were two prisoners in cells, feeling the night air freeze into a trap around yet another life. He lay awake, listening in case she might cry out, with his concern so absorbing it sidetracked the loneliness aching unacknowledged inside of him.

* * * * * *

There was a seductiveness in a suit that changed his perspective on the things around him, a self-confidence that grew when he walked down a polished corridor and heard his gleaming shoes echoing firmly beneath him. The clothes he wore seemed to seal Donal into his new role in life and to exclude the past as if it had happened to a different person. When he had worked and joked and stood among the men on the factory floor their outlook and way of life had seemed an integral part of himself which he could never question or betray. But now that he had stepped outside the confined pulse of that life and had to survive by himself he no longer seemed able to defend the men and their actions as convincingly as before. For a start, the terms of reference were different and the friendship in the office was different from the solidarity of men working as a team for financial bonus. Also, while his superiors were willing to allow him to make the leap from shopfloor to desk they expected it to be a clean break: the person who had voted in the dirty canteen smothered under the bluish-white of his ironed shirt. And as he became preoccupied with the daily concerns of his new position and the issues faded in his mind like caked dirt under constant rinsing, he found that his view and tone in conversation had begun to blend in with the general consensus in the office.

However, the talk among the junior staff in the office rarely touched on the industrial action, as if it were a virus with which they might somehow become infected. Most considered it as an excuse to relax as the tide of work slowed down. One of the clerks had taken Donal by the arm and quietly offered him a lift through the gates if an unofficial picket were placed.

Thursday was pay-day and at lunch time they all went down for soup and rolls in the local lounge. Donal and the two typists had a few gin and tonics and they were in a giggly mood. Both girls were nineteen and shared a flat in Drumcondra. When the cleaning lady brought the coffee around at four o'clock he joined them for his break. There was a sub-language of in-jokes that had evolved in the office which he had begun to grasp and he joined in the discussion of what

106

the girls would do if they got MacCarthy tied to the leg of a chair or what his spinster secretary did at night with her sacred heart lamp.

There was a major meeting in MacCarthy's office and they knew they would not be disturbed so they threw elastic bands and rolls of tape between the desks and sent across notes asking each other outside for one heck of a quickie and three pups and a diddle while they waited for the release of half five. At ten past five agreement was reached between MacCarthy and his board and Toby and the union committee. The status of the women in relation to nights was to remain unchanged, and the men would receive an additional level of bonus for working the blacked wire, equal to the original amount they lost in the first stoppage. Each shift, beginning at half seven on Friday morning, would vote just to ratify it and normal working would resume on Monday morning.

By the time Donal was leaving at half five word had reached the factory and what had been a completely united front began to crumble. By six fifteen first one, and then both, of the operators began to speed up their machines and within half an hour were again working flat-out to try to recoup the bonus money they had lost. The chemicals were churned into flux and bounced up the conveyor belt at twice the normal speed and any breakdown of the machine was cursed as an anxious clot of men gathered around the operator offering advice and checking the time being clicked out by the clock behind them.

When Donal walked past the coils of rusting copper, down past the neat shrubs and out the main gate into the evening traffic on the hill he felt as if a burden had been taken from his shoulders and his final link with the past snapped. Although a part of him felt ashamed he couldn't help feeling a joyful sense of relief. He grinned as he marched down the hill checking the ends of his suit for dirt. He paused at the supermarket where he used to leave Frankie and for a wild moment considered calling over to tell Frankie the news. But he was frightened of what he might find in the bedroom of Barbara's mother's house where the person who had once seemed almost able to get inside his brain now lived like a warning.

* * * * * *

The girl had been lying face downward on the blanket for half an hour with the shoulder straps of her bikini top undone as she allowed the late evening sun to stun her body into a hypnotic state of well-being. Her face was pressed deeply into a pillow and her dark body was stretched out as if it were trying to hug the earth. Without warning she turned over with her right hand automatically reaching across to catch the straps and, glancing up, she caught Dan straight above gazing down at her from his window. The old man's head was too far out for him to duck back and he was stranded there while she glared at him in shock and confusion. Dan backed away from the window sill and sat back on the bed beginning to tremble as he confronted his own humiliation. It all came back to him: standing like an idiot outside a bathroom in Drumcondra when the Donegal girl came out two years ago. And the time in 1971 when the boyfriend had told him to be out of the house on the North Circular Road by the weekend. Drawn to spy as if he could live off the debris of other people's lives. Forced by a compulsion in spite of, or maybe because of, the risks involved. In this life where he had taken so few risks, where his life had flowed like water into any container that would hold it, perhaps whenever he finally built the space around him to call home part of him needed to break the security of the dam and let his life flow on down to the very bottom of the pit.

Certainly he would leave the house sooner than face that girl again. As always, the one thing he cared for he himself had taken away. Some of the girls who passed through would have laughed into his face and forgotten the matter or joked about it to their friends. But this girl, he suspected, came from a place that while probably ultra-modern now had, even in her time, been as backward and ingrown as the village he came from. He shuddered on the bed in the thought that she might still possess the kind of primitive instinct to see beyond the labels the other girls would have placed on him, that he might have exposed himself much more deeply than he had risked doing. There was no way he could ever explain to that girl's face, no way of knowing how much she knew or despised him.

He dreaded having to move again. These things could begin to catch up on him. Each time it became more difficult and expensive to find a new flat. Landlords looked at him with the suspicion that he might die on their hands with no relatives and the last week's rent uncollected. He pressed his forehead against his palms and rocked back on the bed soundlessly as the sun burned down and night like black ash covered over the room. Holy Mary, Mother of God, pray for us now and at the hour of our death. What he had turned into over the years came to him with a force he had never allowed himself to experience before. Like a mask pulled down over his face he had managed to keep the appearance of life alive, but beneath the clothes and job and roof over his head he had been decaying for years, no better than those senile old men he refused to visit or the drunks pestering him in the park. Those nights standing for hours on the landing, hoping the phone would ring for somebody, and when it didn't finally picking it up and dialling a number at random just to hear the voice at the far end breathing and saying over and over "Hello" in a puzzled intimacy before putting the receiver down. Standing in the cubicles of public toilets and reading the scribbled messages of dates and longings and fantasies of desperate men and feeling a glow as if he could draw breath from seeing into their lives.

His mouth was dry, everything he touched felt like the numbness after a dentist's needle. Even his faith had become so perverted that it had become the opposite of what it stood for. A sign he had asked for. A pillar of fire to guide him through the desert into a promised land. His promised land was the brown clay of Glasnevin, the metal teeth of a bulldozer pounding earth over his coffin and an unmarked grave in the shadow of the high wall beside a dual carriageway. And if after that there were a hell it would not be a place of fire and brimstone. It would be having to lie there for eternity in that narrow space and be forced to relive, moment for moment and over and over, all the slow tiny crucifixions of these years and to repeat the tragedies and the mistakes, the hours and days lost in hopelessness, forever, even after the white skull had caved in and only the bones lay twisted like clues to a jigsaw puzzle. That would be the ultimate trick of life, the sealing off of the blank release at the end of his days.

* * * * * *

Elizabeth turned the radio on and the pop jingles were shaken across the garden through the open caravan window with the sharp tinkle of ice-cubes. Her back was turned and neither of them spoke. It had all begun as a piece of playacting. He kept tickling her on the knee whenever she passed and she had jeered at him and said, "You're all talk and no action." Donal grabbed her and pulled her down on his lap on the edge of the chair beside the disused electric fire. She twisted round in his arms: "Well, what are you going to do now?" Laughing as she pulled faces at him. Then when he was silent and just gazed at her she touched his face with her hand and said, "A penny for your thoughts?"

Under her loose summer dress her stomach was huge so that even though she was perched on his knee her body seemed a long way from his. He reached forward towards her on the unsteady chair and lost his balance and suddenly they both fell so that her back banged heavily against the wire guard of the fire. Everywhere he went with Elizabeth they seemed to fall or break things as she rushed excitedly about and she had always grown flustered and then begun to laugh with embarrassment. But this evening even though she had giggled at his panicking over her he could feel the incident hanging between them and their earlier exhiliration wind down into this sulking silence. In the same way as once she flew into laughter, now she could burst into angry red tempers with tears always just behind the pure whiteness of her eyes, her lips pursed and her face burning up into a deep blush. Both of them seemed to be retreating into their private worlds leaving an unspoken void between them which stretched their nerves. Donal knew that both of them desperately wanted to make it up and restore the intimacy and trust they had known, but neither of them as yet seemed to know the words that would break down the sheet of ice that was hardening between them. "Elizabeth, I love you," might have done, but it sounded so trite compared to the emotions racing within him and so cheapened by a million false uses that Donal was afraid it might sound stupid and backfire against him. He knew there had to be more exact words that would liberate his feelings and express fully both his love and his fears to her, but when he looked at her all he could manage was the silence that saved him from the danger of ridicule.

Thursday night was film night and, as if nothing had happened, they both dressed to go out and walked, repeating, tired jokes about the neighbours they passed, down to the queue at the bus stop. Elizabeth had chosen an adventure film and the crowd in the plush darkness of the cinema braced themselves before every onslaught on their nerves. Donal sat in one of the centre rows with his arm held stiffly around Elizabeth's shoulders. He could feel it going asleep on him in its cramped position. In front of him the plot of the film built up and surprised him, but for the first time he found it impossible to abandon himself fully to the screen. After a few moments he began to resent the action that was attempting to create and then manipulate emotions within him. The colours and sounds coming from the screen were like giant invisible fingers reaching through the darkness to play with him

"I'm not ready! I'm not ready!" he wanted to scream at the picture. "Leave my life alone. I can't keep up with you."

He was still nineteen and just a few months ago, like a scene from another old movie, she had stood before him in her green school uniform, catching the pink blossoms of lilac. Now in ten or eleven weeks she would give birth to a stranger who would rule their lives and shape their future for them. And even as he tried to think things out he found his attention and his emotions were still being drawn back into the screen, and that his blood was rising and ebbing in the tide of those sitting enthralled around him. He gave up and gazed ahead, his arm aching with pins and needles, no longer having any control over the future of his life or the flow of his adrenalin.

* * * * * *

Dan didn't know if it had all begun as an accident or if the girl had been waiting there, surrounded by the cold rows of white tiles, knowing that at some stage he would have to leave his room. She had the door slightly ajar and a bathrobe tied loosely around her as if she had just entered the shower when he turned the handle of the door. As he started to open the door he heard the sound of the hot and cold taps being turned on and then a soft thud as if a bare foot had knocked against the shower door by mistake swinging it half open.

He opened the door quietly to sneak out and then, staring across the landing, stopped in shock. He felt his throat turn bone-dry and his whole body began to tremble. The small oriental body moved under the warm jets of water, the soap in a long white foam racing across the dark skin. As she turned towards him he recognised – although smaller than he had imagined and darker than the chipped statue above his bed – the figure that he had been following down through all these barren years. The girl turned towards him fully, bundling up her black hair with both hands into a living jet eucharist above her head, exposing her high neck and shoulder bones to his gaze. The word was made flesh and dwelt . . .

"Mary," he prayed, "this life is so sweet. And though it is too late for me to share its plenty I can still taste it on my tongue. My heaven will be in the black host of her hair, my baptism in the secret smile she will carry away from here."

And in that moment of illumination there came to Dan the sudden sweet drop of disillusion, because he realised that if this girl were Mary, then Mary in turn was just the same as this girl: human and frightened, vulnerable and yet strong enough to risk everything in one terrible step into the unknown, to take on the child of a stranger who appeared in the darkness of a locked room or the cold terrified gaze of an old man. Through the steam rising in grey-white clouds around her he could see the faint stitches of an operation over her stomach and he knew that even she, in all the wild energy of this moment, was also dying. The death he had been running from for all these years was not a black full-stop in the future. It had been occurring within him unnoticed ever since the moment of his birth, in the tiny piece of him that died every time he exposed himself to the blinding rays of life. And now it seemed that it was only in his acceptance of death that he could begin to measure and to understand his life and to appreciate, like a bonus, the few years left to him to open and to be opened, to touch those slowly ageing around him and for his decaying body to be touched, before the warm oblivion they would all be swept into like petals from the tree melting back into the earth.

Dan knew that she could feel his eyes watching her, not now with lust or hunger, but with a sort of helpless surrender. And as her face slowly blushed into a smile it seemed to him that she was washing off these months of suppression and hiding with the white suds that rolled from her body, as if this moment were releasing her like a caged hare and she were discovering the pure freedom of movement again. The girl brushed the drenched strands of hair away from her face as if they were fingers held over frightened eyes and smiled a rich smile of conspiracy at the silent and grave old man whose name she didn't know. Neither of them felt the need to speak. She turned off the hissing jets of water and it was as if the abrupt silence returned them to reality. She placed the bathrobe modestly over her soaking body. He stepped back and closed his door with a gentle click and stood perfectly still in front of its discoloured paintwork for several minutes until his face relaxed into a smile.

They sat late into the night in their separate rooms, and as Dan cleared out the tiny grate of the fireplace intending later to handfeed the contents of his suitcase into it, he could hear the sound of her packing through the thin wall. He heard the impatient ringing of her bell, then the heavy thumping of the old door knocker and finally the thick Mayo accent in the street below calling up to the window and gradually draining in confidence, until a car door slammed and the purr of the engine died away through the darkened streets like a sound of bees retreating through the trees in a summer twilight.

Eight

AS HE woke to the metallic hysteria of the alarm clock there was a sour taste in Donal's mouth and a harsh burning in his stomach like the pain when he used to wake on those afternoons after the night shift. All night he had been blacking out into confused dreams and falling awake again, curled uncomfortably beside Elizabeth in the narrow bunk where their bodies locked into the tides of each other's movements. The blankets had wound up around her shoulders and Donal's limbs were stiff in the cold dawn. He focused his eyes into the sharp light and, pulling a jumper over his head, walked over to put the kettle on and make tea for her.

An undercurrent of tension remained, a hangover from their coldness of the night before, and their conversation was of matter-of-fact arrangements. Neither of them wanted to be the first to yield to open speech again as if they both needed to assert their independence from the other. Donal decided to allow things to hang in the air and let the routine events of the day soften the memory of their meaningless squabble. This evening after work he would find the words to make it up and they would be drawn closer together as if the forgiveness were a renewal of their vows to each other.

There was a festive atmosphere in the office at the ending of the work-to-rule. The more reserved members of the staff seemed more relaxed with him as though some taint had now been removed. At last Donal felt himself fit more easily into this new world he was determined to make his way in. Later in the day, if he got a chance, he would slip down to the factory for a joke and a slag with the lads on the production line. He would have to make sure the new slugger was treating his baby right. For the moment he was content to allow himself to be swallowed up by his work, to lose the jumbled language of his private life in the clean and confident vocabulary of business deadlines and sales figures. He experienced an unexpected sense of pleasure in phoning the customers who had been harassing him to bring forward delivery dates, as if he, by telling them, were somehow responsible for the successful outcome.

By eleven o'clock he was fully hyped-up into his new role of good-news salesman and was relaxing with his tie loose as he enjoyed the coffee and biscuits when MacCarthy's face appeared around the door of the large office from the corridor.

"Donal, phone an ambulance at once!" he snapped and then vanished back down the corridor.

For some reason Donal savoured the chance to finally dial the magic 999 and then, as he was still on his break, he slipped down the corridor to the factory. When he pushed the chipped plywood door open he was surprised by the unnatural hush from the switched-off machines and could hear distinct footsteps resounding towards him. There was a coldness and squalor about the factory, with its rusting metal and decaying paintwork, that he had never noticed when working there. Production had stopped and through the gaps of light between the stacked rows of trays he could see the men crowded in a circle around the foot of the storage bay ladder. Jimmy was walking towards him, shaking his head as he looked down at the concrete path.

"Jimmy, what's happening?"

The small man brushed past Donal as if he didn't know him, his body sagging as he made his way to the jakes. Through the black curtain of men he could see flashes of a kneeling white coat.

"They've killed the scab," he thought, "I don't fucking believe it!"

He pushed his way through the men and almost stepped on Dan's body lying crookedly where it had fallen from the ladder. An image he had buried away in his mind came vividly before his eyes: the group of boys standing casually around the charred carcass of the horse.

The old man turned his head painfully on the ground towards him and whispered something to the company medic who looked up and asked, "Are you Donal?"

"Yes."

"He wants you." The medic nodded with a quick downward flick of his head and then rose from his knees to talk in a low voice to MacCarthy.

Donal knelt as in a dream on the oil-smeared stone floor beside the figure whose whispering was too faint to hear. The circle of men moved back. Donal lowered himself until his ear was beside Dan's lips.

"Donal, please, clear out my flat for me. Burn that suitcase. Don't even look inside it. For God's sake, don't let anybody else find it, especially anyone in the house. Donal, do this one favour for me, please."

The old man moved his hand down slowly to his overall pocket and then pushed the keys into Donal's hand, grasping hold of the young man's palm for a moment before releasing it and turning his face away. The knot of men was beginning to break up and reform in smaller groups to talk in low voices. Donal stood up as the stretcher came in and watched the familiar old blue overalls being carefully lifted and then strapped in and covered by a white sheet. He reached his hand out for support against a rung of the ladder and felt a soft jelly under his fingers. He straightened himself up and gazed at the green grease that traced a thin line across his palm. It was the same as they used to put on the handles of the slugger for a joke.

"Did you know him?" MacCarthy's voice came from behind his shoulder. Donal turned to face him, then looked down at the line of grease again.

"No. None of us did."

Duckarse was fluttering around, nervous in the presence of the manager. He began to herd the men back towards the machines, saying, "Come on lads, there's nothing we can do by standing around here." Donal gripped the rungs of the ladder. The lines of grease became heavier as his hands climbed up. It seemed impossible that the men could have done this and yet here was the evidence.

The forklift driver was sitting on one of the twin shafts of his truck. The man's hands were trembling and his cheeks were the colour of a frozen chicken. His voice shook when he spoke.

"I was loading nails down the packing line and getting that blacked

117

wire out of storage to be used again. I asked him to go up and get my lunch for me. He'd do that sort of thing for you. He'd do it without saying anything, the poor old fucking sod."

"I phoned the police," MacCarthy said. When he looked up at Donal's face he went to put his hand on the young man's shoulder and just remembered himself in time. As he was turning away he said softly, "Take a few minutes, son, if you need them." And then, as if realising that the young man could be useful he added, "Talk to the men; you know them better than I do."

Donal watched the turned back in the grey suit slip quickly out of the factory. When he looked down he found that he was shaking. The initial glow of excited shock was gone and he felt that he was discovering the true meaning of hatred. If he had a gun he would begin shooting. From the top down. MacCarthy who when Milo's kid was knocked down had refused to pass on the message from the hospital. Duckarse whose last words to anybody resigning were to tell him his pay would be docked if he left a minute early. And the men who for all their comradeship had done this. There was an adrenalin pumping through his body that he had never experienced before. He gazed down at the worn conveyor belt running blindly towards him. Jimmy and Milo weren't talking or joking as usual. They lifted the trays off the belt like robots and stacked them on the pallet behind. Then Jimmy, without the sure skill of Dan, began to pump up and haul the full pallet away while Milo loaded the trays himself. How quickly a man's role is taken over. Frankie was leaning against the rapidly emptying hodder with a pile of rods held loosely in his hands. He was the only person in the factory that Donal felt he could talk to.

Donal went over to join him and stooping down gathered up a huge bunch of rods with both hands. He hurled them against the metal back of the hodder and watched them shiver into neat rows down the clinking valley. He released a deep breath and looked across at the distant face of his friend.

"Frankie, how could they fucking well do it? How could they set out to try to hurt a scab or anybody?"

Frankie was rolling two rods lightly between his fingers and gazing across at the ladder without really appearing to see it. Then he looked at Donal and asked in a bewildered voice, "Jesus, how could she do it,

Donal? Barbara says she's going to kick me out if I don't get the head together. Where would I go, Donal? What would I do?"

He was silent for a moment and when he spoke he had half his face turned away again and it was as if he were speaking to himself.

"You know, that night when I went to the Milky Way it was everything I had ever imagined it would be. The world and its mother hanging around and rolling numbers. Every sort of dope for sale and hash cake and wine. And up on the stage there were thirteen or fourteen musicians all jamming together, with this black drummer, completely soaked in sweat, holding them all together with his rhythm. And I was standing there in the middle of that stoned crowd praying that one of them would leave the stage and I could get up in his place. But every time one of them stopped playing my legs would refuse to move and somebody else would climb on instead. So finally I just turned around and walked out and on my way back to the hostel for the first time in my life I sneaked into a peepshow. And I put my guilder into the slot and looked through the little pane of glass in the cabin and there was a mirror so you could see the back of the girl and in it I could see the row of eyes reflected, all staring at her. And I suddenly realised that the girl could see me and she came over dancing and swaying to my window and began to squeeze her breasts up against the glass and I didn't want to watch her but I couldn't leave without insulting her until the shutter came down. Then later back in the hostel this German girl saw my guitar case and asked me about it and I told her I'd just played the Milky Way. We had a few drinks and went back to her room and rolled joint after joint and I began to describe it to her so that by the time I screwed her I believed I'd played there myself.

"Jesus, what am I doing here? I never meant to get Dan. For fuck sake, I understand that poor cunt. I don't even think I really wanted to get the scab. He was just there, unlike MacCarthy or Duckarse and any of the other ones I was too scared to go after. Ah, why couldn't Dan have minded his own business? Why did he have to go around being Florence Nightingale on the side? Nobody else would have touched the scab with a barge pole. And yet, do you know a funny thing – this will make you laugh – I used to even talk to the scab when nobody was looking. He's only a harmless old cunt as well. Ah,

119

I don't fucking care anymore. Nothing they can do to me will be worse than this."

"You fucking did it!" Donal's hands gripped the collar of Frankie's sweatshirt and the pile of rods began to slip in single file on to the concrete with a series of sharp clicks. Donal began to shake Frankie violently.

"You almost fucking killed him, you stupid bastard! And for what? You cunt! You bastard!"

And he screamed at Frankie in a great incoherent stream. At first it was because of the image of the twisted figure lying on the ground and then Donal realised, as if a straight jacket were being burst open, that deep down he had hated Frankie for years without ever acknowledging it. All the buried resentment from childhood began to surface in his mind.

"You've always wanted to keep me down, you fucker. I used to look up to you once. You were my hero and I was just your side-kick. And look where you've led me. But I'm not your side-kick any longer. I've got out of this stinking hole and you'll never drag me back down. I've aped you for too long, but I'm standing in the light now away from your poxy shadow."

And in those moments it seemed that Donal could trace every mistake he had ever made back to Frankie: the blind alleys of all those childhood schemes, those nights on the tear, the months in this factory, his marriage. Even though he knew this was unfair a part of him was wallowing in the release from guilt and the chance to turn his anger against a solid thing. And then he realised that he didn't hate Frankie; what he hated were those aspects of his own personality that he found reflected in the older boy. And as he grasped this he stopped shaking him and stepped back as if afraid that the other's capitulation might somehow be passed on to him. He looked at the glazed and helpless eyes before him and he wasn't even sure if Frankie could hear what he was saying.

Frankie stood there against the empty hodder that had caused the machine to break down and Donal realised that the noise had stopped and the men were silently watching them. All the anger had drained itself out of his body and there was just a vacuum left and the faint memory of pity. The memory of the closeness they once shared came back to him and suddenly Donal had to stop himself taking the silent figure in his arms.

"Ah, Jesus Christ, Frankie. Tell us, mate, what are you on?" he asked.

The light seemed to switch itself back on in Frankie's eyes. A smile came to his lips as if he were imparting a great secret when they were children.

"The best of heroin, kid. Rolling gold through your veins. There is a little door into your mind and it clicks it open and you could never imagine the feeling. Colours are just shooting out of the dark like fireworks. You just come out of yourself and hang there. Come over to the house, Donal, and I'll share it with you. We're mates. You come over. Mate come back."

Donal turned and walked away from the figure beside the hodder, away from the men standing watching him, past Duckarse and through the plywood door. In the corridor MacCarthy was talking to two policemen.

"Donal, did you find out anything in the factory?" he asked.

"I found nothing." The answer was muttered as he walked past to take his place at the desk beside the huge plate glass window and telephone the next customer.

After lunch he was called to MacCarthy's office. In the corridor he met Jimmy returning to the factory.

"Watch them fuckers," he said. "They are trying to play dirty. Oh, did you hear we're losing our shop steward? He's off to Belfast on Monday." The man moved to walk on and the paused again.

"Listen Donal, the boys in blue are after taking Frankie away. You know none of the lads had anything to do with it. It would never be our idea. Give it a week or two and we'll all be hitching rides up and down the factory on the forklift and playing cards with Mick up in the canteen. I had me hands full stopping some of the fellows from tearing your mate apart when they found out. What was he up to at all?"

The two senior executives who had interviewed him for the job were in the office with MacCarthy. This time they spoke to him in confidential management-to-management voices. Dan was recovering in the Mater Hospital. The results of his x-rays were not through

121

yet. Had Donal been a close friend of the man? Had he any known relatives? Did he drink? Was there anything odd in his behaviour? They moved their chairs closer to him, probing softly for anything that might save them the cost of compensation.

Donal stared back at them sullenly and they changed the questions around to Frankie.

"Now, how about this Francis chap? You worked with him as well. The police are questioning him. He appears a bit dazed by the whole affair. Have you any ideas about him?"

"Snots!" Donal said, standing up and looking at MacCarthy.

"What?"

"Will be appearing under your nose!"

Nine

THERE WAS a smell of decay about the house when Donal stepped from the high stone step into the darkened hall which had one wall painted a bright blue and old cream paintwork peeling from the rest of the stonework. Lying at his feet there was a large plain brown envelope with Dan's name in handwriting under an English postmark. He wondered could it be a relative over the water? There was no answer from the flat on the ground floor when he knocked and the key would not fit. As he climbed the stairs to where he could see four doors through the banister the light he had switched on went out with a soft pop throwing the whole house into semi-darkness. One long ray of evening sunlight was spotlighting the dust as it shafted through a crack in the hammered glass pane of the toilet. The cubbyhole beside that contained a makeshift shower. The next door he tried creaked open by itself and he stepped into a small bed-sit where an old picture of a showband covered a damp patch on the wall. Rough blankets were neatly folded at the foot of the single bed, and the empty drawers of the woodwormy press were left open, exposing yellowed newspapers lining the bottom of them. There was an envelope pinned to the white pillow with the name Sergeant William Casey printed in neat handwriting on the front. The window was open and Donal could see a wasteland of weeds and litter through the glass.

The key turned in the lock of the fourth door and Donal gazed into the small flat. Lace curtains dyed brown with dirt were fitted over the window which cast a rippled flow of light across the coloured pattern of lino on the floor. There was a heavy iron bed against the far wall and on a shelf above it a small statue of the Blessed Virgin stood watch over the room. Yellow milk crawled up the edge of a plastic bottle beside the pockmarked white sink. A tiny gas cooker with two rings and a grill was perched on top of the draining board and a jar of fifty pence pieces stood on the mantelpiece beside an old clock. Apart from the wardrobe and a table and single chair that was all Donal could see in the room.

But the thing that impressed itself most on his mind was not the contents but the atmosphere within the unlit room. It retained a musty smell which, although only caused by dampness, frightened Donal as if it were the stench of a crypt. He shivered and went inside, not even sure of what he was supposed to be doing. He wanted to fulfil his promise quickly and not be any later home to Elizabeth than necessary. The shelf with the statue also had three westerns from the library. A few other books lay on top of the wardrobe with an old newspaper covering them. He wiped off the dust with his fingers and read the titles: *The Singer & Other Plays,* a Legion of Mary handbook for 1953, *Morality and the Young Catholic Teenager* by a Fr Thomas O'Brien, S.J., and *The Easter Rising 1916-66, A Souvenir Record of the Celebrations.*

Inside the wardrobe there were two neatly hung suits, one made of heavy cloth in an old-fashioned style and the other more modern and much cheaper looking. A few shirts, all white. Two pairs of shoes and an old Oxo box with polish and brushes. An assortment of vests and underpants and ties and in a cardboard box a few odds and ends including an old hairbrush and a broken alarm clock. On the shelf at the top there was an envelope containing tax forms and other legal documents and a second torn envelope with Dan's name and an address in North Fredrick Street. In this Donal found three references for jobs; one dated Dublin 1934, one from a factory in London in 1947 and one from a Dublin builder, dated 6 February, 1959: " . . . an honest and punctual worker, capable of carrying out all instructions. I can recommend him with no reservations . . . "

Donal remembered one winter night as they had both sat in the cloakroom listening to the rain beating down when Donal had told him where he lived. Dan had asked him who built those houses and when the boy mentioned a company he shook his head, laughing until he reached over and slapped Donal's knee saying, "I did! Me and the men I worked with. We built them with our own hands, boy!"

Yet there was nothing here to show evidence of a life outside his work except for one old photograph of a tall young man standing awkwardly in a country lane in a stiff black suit with a spidery looking old woman stooped over a stick and also dressed completely in black. The whole picture was retreating into a single brown tone and the smudged words on the back were now illegible. There were no letters home, no address book. Even the walls had no mementoes to give the room the sense of being a home. The sole thing that seemed to save it from the bland anonymity of a cheap hotel and link the room with Dan was the atmosphere.

It was only the second time he glanced under the bed impatiently in the evening glow that he noticed the suitcase pressed right back against the wall. He reached underneath and pulled it towards him across the lino. It was an old-fashioned case with Dan's name written on a cardboard B & I sticker attached to the handle. There was little of interest in the top layer as Donal sifted through it: old religious magazines and newspaper cuttings about hurling finals and local events from country papers.

His hand reached underneath the cuttings and brought out a fistful of papers. A girl lay back against a rocking chair with one knee dangling over the arm of it, wearing only a loosened silk blouse and red shoes. Both hands were playing down between her spread legs while her eyes under long straight black hair were closed and dreamy, her lips slightly open and her head thrown right back. The one below was in black and white, a young girl – maybe sixteen or seventeen – lying sideways on a beach. Her bikini top was flooded by long folds of black hair and the picture seemed to be cut from a holiday brochure. Donal emptied the suitcase on to the floor and discovered that there were hundreds of them. He pulled the cord above his head and gradually from the twilight a long single bar of red heat emerged above him. As he began to spread more of the pictures over the floor he could notice the similarities between them, the constant black hair, long and straight, the downward look of the eyes and the half smile. It was like building a photofit picture of a missing person in a police station. Yet the ages and the positions ranged from the innocent to the horrific. He found the initial M scribbled over one or two of the

125

photographs.

When he first began to sift through the pictures the distant symptoms of desire had started to stir like an automatic mechanism through his body. Yet when he worked his way through the stronger poses and young models a wave of disgust overcame it. That little girl in the blue dress, could she be more than twelve or thirteen? The schoolgirl with jeans down receiving the cane from the grey-bearded teacher, so posed and unreal. And even more frightening the stills from films, the obviously real pain of skin blistering red and turning to blue ugly blotches. There was nothing in these pictures of life; they spoke to him only of fear and of hatred. The only desire in them was to crush all growth, to destroy what they themselves could not enjoy, to pervert all humanity and life out of existence.

Pervert! The word came to his tongue like a dirty raincoat that he could never imagine Dan wearing. Junkie! The role of a bit-character in the credits of a B-movie that he could not imagine Frankie acting in. Yet the titles and the roles had to fit.

"Stay away from them fellows upstairs. They're only dirt. They'll pollute you." The old man's soft Galway accent came back to mock him. Dan with his slow genteel walk and his air of sad dignity, coming home to live out of this suitcase. None of these pictures seemed to have come from the same magazine. This was no casual hobby or fad. This was pure obsession.

Donal found that his gaze had wandered up and was resting on the vaguely familiar features of the statue above the bed. He sat back puzzled by it for a long time before his mind finally grasped the connection. He took down the statue, with hands stretching down under the blue robes, and placed the Queen of Heaven and the Star of the Sea in the centre of the floor among the jumbled likenesses of her children.

Across the back gardens that backed on to the house the woman was about to pull the blind down when she gazed through her window. There was that man again as usual, a dark outline in the soft red light of the window. She often wondered about him, just sitting there like that for hours without moving, gazing down at the ground like a statue. With a quick jerk of the cord she snapped the blind shut.

126

* * * * * *

Donal was glad to be out in the night air again. He walked down towards Phibsboro Corner into the excitement of a Friday night. Behind him the last ashes were still faintly glowing in the dark room. It had taken him over an hour to feed the pile of papers into the tiny fireplace. He had knelt beside the grate watching the pictures being consumed one by one, the edges of each photograph turning brown and curling up and then the sudden tentative lick of flame spreading along the legs or across the face of the model trapped in her pose. A thousand likenesses, gathered together over decades, finally becoming one in the drumlin of blackened ash growing in the fireplace. The keys he had placed in a brown envelope and meant to give in to the night porter at the Mater Hospital, but the long curving flight of steps up to the floodlit locked doors of the building seemed intimidating and he decided to do it tomorrow in the daylight. Anyway he felt too confused to talk to anyone. He stood outside looking through the railings at the dark shrubs and the fake celtic cross in the small park and tried to calm himself. But after the slow feeding of pictures into the fire his mind was bombarded with images of pain and humiliation and in the centre of it all, flashing across his mind over the dark peacefulness of the locked park, was the bent shape of Dan lying on the concrete floor and the drugged, smiling face of Frankie calling after him from the hodder. Donal turned away and walked down past the crumbling buildings of Eccles Street towards town.

Within minutes he found himself being carried down the brightly lit river of O'Connell Street, while on both sides of him the crowds in their weekend fashions were pouring out from the cinemas and jamming the pubs and plate-glass hamburger joints. He walked down the traffic island under the trees in the centre, cut off from the pavements by the streaming cars on either side. At the pedestrian lights a tiny girl around thirteen in ankle-length parallels and black jacket came out from under the shadow of a statue. She rocked her small hips suggestively.

"Mister, you know where I can score some heroin? I'll make it worth your while, so I will, Mister."

127

He shook his head and crossed the street to where a group of dirty children were standing outside an American burger house, holding black plastic bags to their faces and breathing in. They swayed through the path of the crowd, begging and cursing and giggling. It seemed to him that their entire world must be compressed inside that black bag of glue which expanded inside their minds into a universe of colour. The eldest girl took hold of one young boy's shoulders and pressed him tenderly against the plate glass window until his stupor passed and he could walk again. The other children defensively formed into an unsteady circle around them. A boy dressed in a sawn-off communion suit blocked Donal's path saying, "You're a great man, Mister, a great man altogether," as his hands tried quickly to explore his pockets. Donal shrugged him off and the children set out groggily towards the quays, weaving through the swell of bodies, slipping and pushing against people.

He stood to watch a pair of them race through the traffic laughing and begin to kick at the cars clustered in a knot at the traffic lights on O'Connell Bridge. The children pressed their faces against the glass as they banged on the roof, watching the faces change from indifference through fear into hatred. The lights turned green and the cars moved off with a jerk and tore up O'Connell Street as the children ran behind shouting after them.

Donal paused for directions on O'Connell Bridge and realised that he had nowhere to go. It was the first time he had ever stood in the centre of the city at night when he wasn't drinking with Frankie or at the pictures with Elizabeth or some other girl or rushing to keep an appointment. He never before had time to pause and examine the place. There were so many changes from his childhood that he could hardly recognise some of the streets. He had grown up in this city and yet had never really bothered to examine it and now it was moving past him and he felt strangely homeless. As he stared at the new neon displays over the fast food huts and video arcades he seemed no longer certain of the sense of place he had taken for granted. Flourescent advertisements chased their tails up and down the sides of buildings, spelling out their messages around him. He stood on the bridge and could see that the pale blue dome of the night sky and the soft pastel shades of the summer clothes were like an invisible cocoon around the crowd – just like the children's bag of glue or the drivers' breathing in the drug of speed and of comfort in their bubbles of chrome. Like those passing girls who would pay with turned backs for the spent glue-coloured sheath in the cold dawn. Like Dan's treasure trove of pictures or Frankie's golden incision into his veins. And just the same for him stapled into his desk beside the large windows by the inverted freedom of his wage packet. For all of them the price of sleep would constantly be high.

Though the city had lived through no recent war the quays looked as if they had been bombed. The refugee children moved past the derelict fronts of buildings that had been left standing like the set from a film along the waterside. Two giant cranes rose above the crumbling facades and dissected the sky with their powerful steel arcs.

The pubs were starting to empty and the streets to fill up with noise and danger. Along the quays long lines of couples queued to kiss under the yellow lights and coloured flags above the bus shelters. Like a squadron of fighter pilots the bus crews scrambled from the bars and the convoy of last buses pulled away from the stops together. The stranded latecomers stopped running and cursed as they made for the taxi ranks. A skinhead chased his mate down the street shouting and, lunging from behind, hit him with a flying kick on the shoulder: both fell laughing and rolling over on the pavement together. Two young boys hid behind a car in Westmoreland Street while the child-girls they had chatted-up stood with puzzled expressions at the corner of Fleet Street where the crowds queued for the discos. In a doorway a tramp lay asleep or dead with the sodden multi-coloured crumble of vomit beside him. Across the road a tiny girl in bright pedal-pushers tried to separate a pair of boys kicking each other against the side of a parked van. There was laughter and fear and pop music and the swirl of headlights in the air.

Donal joined the queue for food in one of the hamburger joints where the girls in gaudily striped jackets and paper hats called the orders into microphones while behind them the boys worked the massive grills and ovens. Half-drunk customers queued and cuddled in discomfort under the watchful eyes of the bouncers at the door. The eyes of the small, dark girl with black cropped hair who served him were blank as she bounced around the counter, jabbing at the

129

cash register with one finger and jumping back from it, singing to herself. She seemed oblivious to everything but the figures printed up on the cash machine.

Donal sat at one of the plastic tables and thought of his own obsessions, the silly childish illusions that he had hauled around like old dirty postcards. Once he had believed there was a single moment when you crossed the threshold out from the mistakes and fears of adolescence into the certainty of manhood. But now it seemed that there were hundreds of moments instead when life, like a mafia godfather, demanded the surrender of yet another piece of yourself as the price of survival and acceptance.

A fight started behind him as he was eating and the bouncers moved in quickly. The two youths were separated and thrown out into the street to finish it there. Donal could feel a tense, sullen expectation behind the laughter and knew that just one look or push or the suspicion of a remark was enough to ignite the frayed and frustrated tempers.

He was glad to escape to the street outside where young girls were passing, clapping their hands in time and singing love songs. Their faces were alive with drink and happiness. He had known such carefreeness with Elizabeth before their lives had begun to move faster and faster like a landslide down a mountain. And somewhere in the centre of that avalanche they were two pebbles which had been jolted apart and were trying to scramble back to each other: two children who had joined together in a play marriage that had become reality. Like Frankie before him he had the choices to make and finally had to face up to himself. All the fears and decisions he had suppressed erupted as his feet aimlessly led him through the streets, until the late-night films ended and the dancehalls and discos evicted their patrons, until the fleets of taxis swept the revellers away and, in the matter of a few minutes, the city grew quite again.

It was the hour when the night tide turned, when the lovers were gone and only the victims remained. Donal turned for home through streets where his footsteps echoed up towards the rooftops of the dark buildings. Under the floodlit portals of the Central Bank a girl was sobbing hysterically as the man who was half holding her up glanced around for a means of escape.

130

"But you don't understand, Johnny! Nobody understands! Give me a minute to explain! A minute for Jesus sake, Johnny! Johnny! Johnny!"

Her words amplified by her drunken anguish followed Donal as they began to walk behind him. As with an over-excited child the sentences became alternated with tears. Donal thought of the five repressed days leading up to the ultimatum of the weekend: Thou shalt enjoy! The couples falling over each other, drunk and gaily singing on the plush seats of the lounge bars, released from responsibility by alcohol to pledge themselves to emotions they would have forgotten by the morning. The white-shirted barmen lined up observing and calculating: after a few drinks upturning the empty glasses in a stale saucer of gin before pouring in the ice, tonic and sparkle of lemon, the familiar taste of alcohol along the rim convincing the mind eager for an excuse.

"You don't understand, Johnny! I just don't know what's wrong! Wait for me, Johnny! Oh Jesus, Johnny, Johnny, please!"

On the steps of a building beside the National Ballroom a woman in her early thirties sat with an older man's head in her lap. His tie was undone and his eyes closed. Apart from the faint restlessness of her fingers loitering uncertainly in his hair they might have been a statue. A girl with tousled brown hair looked up outside the undertakers in North Frederick Street. She smiled at him and said in a Mayo accent, "I'm locked out of my hostel. You're a nice looking fellow. Have you a bed for the night?"

Donal shook his head and as her head dropped her eyes went out like the lights in a building. He watched her shuffle in her duffle coat down towards town, ready to give herself to the next man willing to pretend. The lines of vomit and urine were less frequent as he moved further away from the centre of the city. A scream rose from the corner of Dorset Street. The man eating chips on the step didn't look up.

Donal hailed a taxi that was stopped at the traffic lights. The driver was a stocky middle-aged Dubliner who offered him a cigarette and asked, "You all alone, mate?"

Donal nodded, gazing ahead through the windscreen.

"Well, you won't hear me complain. It makes a nice change, I can

131

tell you, on a Friday night. The money is great at the weekend, but Holy James Street, I'm sick of working it. Tell us this, do you ever see all those couples lined up down the quays at the weekend, kissing and cuddling like they were lovers for life? Would you believe this now if I told it to you? Over half of them that get into the back seat there manage to concoct a fight somewhere on the way home. I'm sick of listening to them. Every bleeding weekend. And it isn't over a bit of the other, who's sleeping with who. Sure, I wouldn't mind that. That's only natural. No, it's over some petty little thing. He has either been paying too much attention to her friend in the pub or she's after been giving some bloke the glad eye. Anyway, ten minutes after they've been kissing and cuddling down by the quays, they're screaming and shouting at each other in the back of my taxi. It's the drink does it, of course, none of them can handle it. And they all want to show off how they can polish off eight or nine shorts. They're trying to run before they can walk. It just isn't on. Well, the gist of it is that there is one of them roaring at me to stop the car and the other shouting to drive on. 'Now, listen here,' I say to them, 'will whichever one of you is paying for this cab tell me where you want to go and the other one just sit down and shut up . . . ?'"

The rough Dublin voice droned on in the air thick with cigarette smoke. On the dashboard a pirate station was playing non-stop music. A saxophone sent a tingle down his body. Donal eased himself back into the seat and watched the film of streets playing backwards in the rear-view mirror. Maybe it was just his exhaustion but the night outside seemed to press down on the cab like a heavy transparent iceberg. And here he was trapped inside his tiny air pocket of doubt. He still didn't understand it as yet, but he knew that he had to shatter that freezing cube to be able to breathe freely again.

He paid off the taxi near the park and climbed over the railings to try and clear his head by walking the final few hundred yards home. The moon, veiled by clouds, added a grey tint to the soft cushion of grass. It reminded him of the night he spent here with Elizabeth last summer. When he closed his eyes he could still see their coats spread under the trees and feel the tender trust within her body. He realised now that the last thing that tied him down was the only thing he cared for any more. He no longer wanted her as the young schoolgirl she was then. He needed her now as a woman, as an equal to share the things he was experiencing. Hurrying, he climbed out from the dark crater of grass and landed with a loud thud on the pavement at the corner of her street.

"Hello, you there! What's your name?" The country accent came from a dark car from within which the glare of a flashlight had been suddenly turned on him. Donal stood still in shock.

"What?"

"I said, what's your name? Who are you? Where do you think you're off to at this hour of the night?"

"I'm going home. Where do you think I'm going — Butlin's holiday camp?"

"Don't you be getting fresh with me now, sonny. We'll be having your name first."

Donal shielded his eyes with his hand to try and see past the flashlight into the car. He felt deflated and a fresh anger was rising in him.

"Listen, I live down the road. I'm just going home. It's none of your business."

"I asked you a question, son, and I'll get an answer out of you. Now, what's your name?"

Donal turned his eyes away from the glare of the flashlight and used the only weapon he had — his silence. He stayed silent when they put him in the back of the car. He could feel the iceberg stiffening in the wind blowing in the window. He stared dumbly at them when the two policemen stood over him in the small room in the station. This was the test of his independence as a person. They threw questions at him endlessly, one taking over when the other lost his temper. Where was he? Was he at a party? Was he taking drugs? Were there women there? Had he scored? Had he been in a car that night? And always it came back to — what's your name?

The tallest of the policemen stood behind his chair and leaned down until his lips were against Donal's ear. The level of his voice suddenly shot up.

"Do you think you're a smart arse, sonny? I can strip search you, you know. How would you fancy standing there stark naked and getting a surgical glove up the arse?"

133

"What's this, a porno show?" Donal finally broke his silence.

"Well, I've had enough of you now. I've wasted enough time here. John, go down and get a wet towel and knot it tightly. That will leave no marks. Now, what's your name?"

His resistence suddenly caved in as he realised the futility of what he was doing. Even if he tried to explain to the two policemen he knew he would be talking a different language. He was tired of the whole pantomime. He just wanted to be with his wife.

"Donal Flynn."

He answered the rest of their routine questions quietly.

"Well, there you are, son," the tall policeman said, as if he had scored some form of personal victory. "You weren't that tough after all, you crowd never are. Now go on, go home, get out of me sight."

In the corridor outside a man stood with his fingers over a gash on his forehead. Blood was trickling through and forming a small stain on the waxed floor. In the first hints of light over the gravel carpark two motorbikes were parked, their radios conversing in crackled tones across the silence that Donal stepped through.

Ten

WHEN DONAL reached the front door of the house dawn was filtering soft light through the branches of the trees on the roadway outside. He wondered would Elizabeth be awake for him like she used to be when he came home from the night shift. He had some explaining to do, but now he felt he knew the words and had found the strength to say them. He tiptoed through the silent house and opened the caravan door with a sense of homecoming he had not known before. The narrow bed had not been slept in. Donal stared in incomprehension at the neatly tucked-up blankets over the unwrinkled sheets and then decided that she must be sleeping in her old bedroom. He walked back along the gravel path and crept up the stairs, trying to remember which steps creaked. That bed was also empty. A cold panic within him was being held back by a feeling of jaded disbelief. He paused outside her mother's door for a moment, as if trying to postpone the outcome. Then he knocked softly and, when there was no reply, turned the handle. The bedclothes were flung back and when he touched the sheet it still maintained the memory of warmth. The room was empty. Next door in the box room young Johnny slept soundly. Donal felt too much an outsider to wake him and was too scared of what the boy might have to tell. He went back and searched every corner of the caravan and then the house for a note or any sign of his wife.

Eventually he found himself drawn back to Elizabeth's old bedroom. He lay on the bed that had always been kept made since her marriage. Around him were stacked all the souvenirs of her past: the old ragged teddy bear in the corner, the childhood holiday snapshots taken in Skerries and Bray when her father was alive, the old dresses hung like shadows of her presence in the wardrobe. All the years of her life spent in this room in which he had no part, those photographs of buckets and spades and sand and pony rides and ice cream, of little girl tears and dodgem rides that excluded him. He lay back exhausted on the bed, fingering the pillow where her head had once lain, and despite himself he slept until he was woken by the sound of the front door opening and footsteps in the hall. It was ten past six on his watch. He crept to the landing and looking over the banister saw the figure of a small countryman standing in the doorway. The figure looked up and Donal shivered under a gaze of silent accusation that seemed to say he was an intruder on the scene. Before he looked down he knew that Elizabeth's mother would be standing in the kitchen doorway. She stood without moving below him in her blue hat and overcoat looking at the man whom Donal now recognised from the wedding as Elizabeth's uncle who drove a taxi in Dundrum.

The man said to her, "I'll leave you here now, Mary. Try and get some rest and phone me later in the morning."

Then he turned and walked towards the gate without looking back. Donal felt his anxiety carrying him down the stairs towards the waiting woman in the hallway. Each footstep was like a dreaded descent into a nightmare.

"Where's my wife?" he asked in a low voice.

"So you've decided to come home, have you, after all your gallivanting around? Sure, do you care where she is at all? Do you care that she was up and down the house all night since six o'clock yesterday sick with the worry about you?"

And then the angry tone left her voice as if she hadn't the energy to be upset any more. Her face seemed to become older and more worn in a few seconds. She turned away to walk into the kitchen and sat wearily at the table facing the back window.

"Donal, she's after losing her wee baby. Holy Mother of God, Donal, she's after losing it on you. She was here all evening, child, waiting for you to come home from work. At first she got really cross with you – you know how she can get in a right temper – and then after a bit she began to get real worried. Were you after falling out or what? Every few minutes she would be going out to the front door or the curtains in the sitting room and looking down the street for you. Then when it got very late she wouldn't go down to the caravan by herself and was sitting down here half asleep on the sofa with the little dot still on after the programmes finished on the telly. Around one o'clock I went down and I made her come up and get into the bed beside me. She frightened me, son, just sitting there with a deranged look about her as if she was talking to somebody else I couldn't see in the room. Mother of God, Donal, what were you doing that you didn't know she'd be here waiting for you?"

She stopped talking and her head slowly dropped towards the formica tabletop. Standing behind her bent shoulders Donal wanted to put his arms around her and realised that they had never been close. Despite months of living on top of one another they had never come to know much about each other. He gripped the back of the chair and tried desperately to think of the words of prayers he had long ago forgotten. In his mind he was trying to make bargains with God before the woman could begin talking again.

"Make us a cup of tea, Donal. Make it strong, son. I could use one badly. I had fallen asleep when it happened. I thought that she had too. She was so still and quiet beside me in the bed that apart from the faint sound of her breath you'd swear she was a doll. She must have imagined that she heard you come in the door during the night. It was the awful crash that woke me. I put my hand out and she was gone. The poor child must still have been half asleep. I went out to the landing, Donal, and she was after falling down the stairs in the dark. Lord Almighty, I'll never forget the sight when I turned the light on of her lying there crumpled in her nightdress like she was dead. She has a couple of ribs broken and bruises and she's after losing a lot of blood. It was only a miracle she wasn't killed. But the baby, Donal, the wee stillborn child is gone from her."

She was crying and only appeared to notice when the tears trickled into her mouth. She traced her palms slowly up to her eyes. Donal moved past her to fill the kettle in the sink as the full light of the morning sun glared against the window-pane. He gazed out towards the empty caravan and told himself it was the sunlight shimmering off the aluminium roof that was causing his eyes to water.

* * * * * *

In the corridor outside her ward there was the disinfected smell of hospital life and the distant echo of footsteps from other sections of the unit. When Donal told the nurse on duty who he was she was immediately consoling and cheering and, after offering him tea, led him to Elizabeth's door. Yet behind her professional kindness, he felt that she, and everybody else they passed, was watching and condemning him for what had happened. The nurse opened the door and whispered to him, "She's on sedatives. It might be wiser not to try and wake her after what she's been through, Mr Flynn."

The other bed in the small ward was empty and so she had the room to herself. Donal stood in the doorway before her sleeping body, feeling, under the concerned eyes of the nurse, once more like a stranger who had intruded upon an intimate scene. There was a white bandage over Elizabeth's forehead which lost itself under the golden folds of her hair. Although her face was white it seemed somehow to have regained all of its childlike beauty. The total absorption of her body in sleep reminded him of those first mornings when he had been ashamed to wake her, and the memory was comforting as if the link could make everything the same again. Then he looked down her body and saw how the wrist of her left hand was attached to a tiny drip hung above the bed and noticed the crude knotted rosary that her mother must have placed around her neck. And he felt that not only had he lost his child, but he had lost Elizabeth as well, in different ways to two different forces. He could feel nothing except a dull and wasted sense of loss.

"Perhaps if you were to wait for a few hours, Mr Flynn, your wife might be awake. What she needs most now is sleep."

The nurse spoke softly behind him and as he turned away he could hear her quietly and firmly closing the door. The morning sun gleaming down the length of the scrubbed corridor hurt his eyes as he moved unsteadily towards the exit.

He spent the remainder of the morning sitting on one of the long benches in the Garden of Remembrance among the Saturday crowds. Constantly in his mind the events of the previous night and all the tiny

138

incidents of their few months together repeated themselves: the times the day before when he could have gone home, the moments in the past when he had held himself back from speaking, his helplessness beside her body trembling with tears in the night. Now that it was too late the right words and actions seemed obvious. And suddenly, with the child gone, the future stretched like an aching void before him.

At two o'clock when he came back she was still drugged and Donal wasn't even sure if she was aware of his presence. She lay still in the bed with her eyes opening slightly every few seconds and then closing again as if she were exhausted by the effort. He held her hand and sat beside her for an hour until she fell into a heavy sleep again. The last time he had eaten was in the hamburger joint the night before and his hands trembled holding the knife and fork as he forced himself to eat something in the grill in Parnell Square. When he returned at half five she was conscious, although still groggy, but her entire family was gathered around her: her two brothers and their wives, her Uncle Peter and her mother, joining in the closed circle of family references and jokes he couldn't follow. Elizabeth grasped him by the neck and kissed him as if fearful that something had happened to him. Then she sank back tired against the pillow and took his hand. There was so much he needed to say to her, but her family, while polite to him, made no effort to move back and it was impossible to say the words in their presence. All he could do was whisper "I love you" in her ear and make stilted conversation. Long after the nurse had rung the bell and asked all visitors to leave they were still sitting there, and in the end, it was Donal who had to leave first.

He could not bear the prospect of returning to the caravan alone and, as he left the hospital, discovered the keys to Dan's flat still in his pocket. He spent the evening sitting by himself among the bright clamour of glasses and raised voices in The Hut pub beside Phibsboro Corner and when he was, in turn, evicted from there, walked slowly up towards the flat. He undressed and lay awake in the darkness listening like a thief to the night life in the decaying house. Again and again he tried to tell himself that he had lost her, that nothing could ever be the same again, but his mind was incapable of accepting it. When occasionally in his exhaustion he blacked out into sleep he dreamed that he was still awake and there was a brooding figure watching over him in the darkness of the flat. He would wake fearfully with his eyes scanning the corners of the small room.

Dawn had almost broken before tiredness overcame his nerves and he sank into a heavy sleep. For a while a confusion of vivid images from the past two days clung inside his mind like photographs and then the familiar sensation of falling occured that he had so often fought in the past. But this time he didn't jerk awake and the fall continued until, as if he had been loosened from something, he felt his body floating upward. As his limbs became saturated inside an intense wave of heat he gazed down and could see the streets where he had played out his childhood, and in the centre of the rows of houses the small park beside Elizabeth's home. He seemed to swoop lower until all he could see was that fresh green hollow and across the dew-drenched grass the figure of Elizabeth came running in a white nightdress with beside her, also in white, a young fair-haired child whom he knew to be his dead daughter. They were both laughing to each other and he was wondering what they were running towards when he heard the music rising up above the park. At first he wasn't sure where it was coming from and then he appeared to be pushed upward again so that he could see the long rows of houses all laid out around the park like seats in a concert hall. Although the streets were deserted the windows of every house were wide open and the music was pouring out from each of them in one symphony that was common to them all. And occluded above it he listened until, without warning, he fell and called Elizabeth's name through the sleeping house as he woke and the soaking fever of warmth drained from his body and he lay, eyes open, frightened and convinced he was not alone.

He arrived early at the hospital and slipped straight into her room without speaking to anybody. Elizabeth's face lit up in the bed when he opened the door and as he saw her old spontaneous smile he told himself that, after all, everything would be all right again. He stood there for a moment burdened down under a huge bunch of flowers, feeling his eyes fill up with water, and then ran to the bed and embraced her.

"I've missed you, Donal," she said, "Oh, how I've missed you. I hate this room so much, you know how I always hated small spaces. Let's go for a walk. I'm not supposed to get out of bed but I think I can."

She pulled the bedclothes back slowly and carefully placed her feet into the slippers beside the bed. Donal held out his hand to help her up, but she waved it away, rising, a bit shakily at first, and putting a large blue hospital gown over her nightdress. Then she allowed herself to lean on him as they made their way slowly out into the corridor under the eyes of the nurse on duty in her glass partition. He was amazed that he had forgotten how soft her body was as he tried to get a firm hold of her shoulder under the massive folds of the gown. They moved slowly, counting the steps down the corridor, like people learning how to walk again. At the window at the end of the corridor they stopped and gazed at the scene below them. She had sunk back against him so that most of her weight was borne by his shoulder.

"The only thing that matters, Elizabeth," he said, "is that you are all right. I couldn't have lived if anything had happened to you. Don't mind about the child. Maybe this one just wasn't meant. But we'll have others. Hundreds of them, until you're going around like the old woman who lived in the shoe. I promise you, love. Just tell me that you're okay."

She didn't seem to have heard what he said. She was silent for a moment and then she turned her head to look up at him and when she finally spoke the words came slowly and carefully as if they had been rehearsed.

"It's been a long time since I was able to think this clearly, Donal. Once everything was very simple and I was able to see things but these last few months have all been a blur. I've been lying in this hospital thinking all night and it's all so clear and so cold now. You know, I never thought I'd see you again, Donal. I don't just mean on Friday. I mean every morning and every night you went outside that caravan. Ever since that night I told you I was pregnant and I could see the horror come into your eyes. I was never sure if I would ever see you again."

She rested her head back on his shoulder and he stroked her hair, so dazzling in the sunlight taking hold of it at the window. His voice was anxious and hurt, like a little boy accused in the wrong.

"But I always came back, Elizabeth. You knew that I would always come back to you. If I had to crawl on my hands and knees I'd

141

come back to you."

She was quiet for a long time and seemed to be absorbed in watching the birds searching for crumbs on the low roof below them. He squeezed her shoulder as if seeking reassurance. When she didn't look up he ran his fingers gently up her cheeks to her eyes.

"You're too late, Donal. I've no tears left. I've nothing left. I've cried them all on nights when you were not there and in places you never saw. And now I'm dry. I'm so cold inside and dry and hard. You see, you never came back to me. Oh, you tried hard and you think you did, but you were never able to give yourself fully to me. You loved me and you worried about me, but you never understood me as a person. You could only ever think of me in terms of how I affected you. I stood it for months, Donal, because I loved you so deeply, just waiting for you to do something, to come to some decision about us on your own, but you never could. You just drifted. We were like children playing beyond our depth and I waited for you because, you see, I thought that you knew the next move, but you didn't. I still love you, Donal, but can't you see that I just don't feel clean with you anymore? I need to know beyond any doubt that the man who takes me for his wife does so because of what I am and for no other reason. Donal, I'm sorry, I can't breathe beside you anymore. I need time, maybe I need forever. Please, Donal, just go away now and give me room to become a person again and not some little schoolgirl in a puppet show."

She twisted her body away so that his hand fell from her shoulder and turned to gaze down the corridor to where her mother and the nurse were watching them. She seemed to be fidgeting with her fingers in distress. Her voice, when she spoke again, was older and different, as if she were addressing a stranger.

"You're a lovely man, Donal. I'm sorry. You know I never planned for it to happen this way. I was lying there in the darkness beside my mother thinking about what it would be like if you didn't come back and maybe even if you did come back. I suppose that deep down a part of me had been thinking of doing it from the very beginning, but I still believed in you then and anyway in those days I would never have had the desperation or the courage. Isn't it strange how little we know about ourselves and what we are capable of doing?

142

On Friday night I just didn't care what happened to me anymore. I didn't care – I might even have been glad – if I broke my neck. All I knew was that suddenly I just could not go through with it. You cannot simply ignore a mistake and expect it to go away. And that is what we were. We stood up to nobody. We were steamrollered all the way. But my life isn't over yet, Donal. I'm only eighteen: my life is only beginning. God knows, Donal, I'm not proud of what I did, and my body now is aching for that child; I'm not proud of it, but I'm not ashamed of it either. Because at least I did something. It may have been something wrong, but at least I did it. And in one way I did it for you, Donal. I did it for you because I don't want you tied to me by anything. Maybe I even did it for the child because of the poxy life we would have given it. But much more importantly, lying there in the darkness, half crazy with worry and fear and unable to even think straight, I did it for my sake. And now I've done it and it's for me alone to live with."

And with those words she left the window-sill and started to walk slowly and painfully away from him, never looking back, down the shining corridor towards her mother waiting in her overcoat and blue hat beside the starched clinical uniform of the nurse on duty.

Donal looked down and there on the window sill, diminished by the white sheen of the gloss paint, was Elizabeth's wedding ring. It lay like a third eye that he had tried to see through, an eye he had grown to rely on so much that he had forgotten how to trust his own imperfect vision. And now, with one movement, the pupil had been removed and only the white sheen stared blindly back at him. His knuckle was sore and stiff as he forced the ring over it and placed it beside hers on the sill. Alongside them he put the keys to the front door of the house and the caravan, neatly bound by the company key ring, and then, from his breast pocket, he took the company pen with the logo engraved in gold on the clip and let it drop beside the rest. Through the open window the reggae beat of music came from the radio of the girls sitting on the grass outside. The corridor behind him was filling up with visitors: hubands with bunches of flowers, children being dragged along clutching white envelopes, smiling old people eager to see their new grandchildren. Sunlight blazed against his back through the panes of glass highlighting his shadow on the polished floor. Elizabeth's brother and his wife had joined her mother beside the nurse. He watched the huddled shoulders of the anxious relatives vanish down the corridor between the wards and waited, but nobody nodded. Hesitantly, he began to walk.